OLD LOVER'S GHOST

OLD LOVER'S GHOST

Joan Smith

Chivers Press ● Thorndike Press
Bath, Avon, England ● Thorndike, Maine USA

This Large Print edition is published by Chivers Press, England, and by Thorndike Press, USA.

Published in 1995 in the U.K. by arrangement with Ballantine Books, a division of Random House, Inc.

Published in 1995 in the U.S. by arrangement with Ballantine Books, a division of Random House, Inc.

U.K. Hardcover ISBN 0–7451–2958–7 (Chivers Large Print)
U.S. Softcover   ISBN 0–7862–0301–3 (General Series Edition)

The text of this Large Print edition is unabridged.
Other aspects of the book may vary from the original edition.

Set in 16 pt. New Times Roman.

Printed in Great Britain on acid-free paper.

British Library Cataloguing in Publication Data available

Library of Congress Cataloging-in-Publication Data

Smith, Joan, 1938–
  Old lover's ghost / Joan Smith.
    p.   cm.
  ISBN 0–7862–0301–3 (lg. print: lsc)
  1. Large type books. I. Title.
[PR9199.3.S5515704 1994]
813′.54—dc20
                                    94–28314

CHAPTER ONE

Mr Wainwright came into the saloon, pinching back a smile as he glanced at a letter in his hand. His daughter, Charity, noticed the letter was franked and stifled a sigh of regret. Another visit! Papa could never refuse an invitation to a noble estate. They had just recently returned from Woburn Abbey, the county seat of the Duke of Bedford. Charity had been looking forward to the pleasures of a spring under her own more modest roof in London, with some conversation and activities that did not involve the spirit world.

'Another visit, Papa?' she asked.

'Not just any visit,' he replied, his dark eyes gleaming with excitement. At sixty, the air of a young man still lingered about him despite his silver hair. A pair of jet-black eyebrows and a healthy complexion added to the impression. A jacket of the finest material and cut enhanced the elegance of a tall, lean physique. Mr Wainwright took a keen interest in his appearance. It was his mania for these visits that accounted for it, of course. One could not be hobnobbing with dukes and earls looking like a scarecrow. As the visits kept Papa in curl, Charity refrained from discouraging them.

'Where is it to be this time?' she asked, trying for an air of enthusiasm.

1

'Guess!' he said playfully. 'It will test your psychical powers.'

'Not Longleat!' she exclaimed. Psychical powers had nothing to do with this guess. Papa had been angling for an invitation to Longleat forever.

'Better!'

'I had not thought there was any house you would like better than Longleat.'

'If there is one, it would have to be Keefer Hall. As Lord Merton takes no interest in the spirit world, I had given up hoping for it.'

'And now you have been invited. Why, you are becoming famous, Papa.'

The beaming smile that shone forth through his air of feigned modesty was well worth her burst of exaggeration. 'I daresay my reputation is beginning to spread a little. A nuisance, but one has a duty to share his gifts. I thought it would have been my latest article that caught the countess's interest. It is the countess who has invited me, but of course Lord Merton would be aware of it—approve. My treatise on the ghost of Radley Hall was widely circulated and well received. There is nothing like the death of a beautiful young woman to catch folks' interest. It was not the article that did it, however. It seems Lady Montagu put her on to me. My work with the brown monk at Beaulieu convinced Lady Montagu of my peculiar talents. I got the fellow to stick to the ruined cloisters of the old abbey, as that is what Her

Ladyship wished.'

'Yes, Papa, I remember Beaulieu very well,' his daughter replied. 'And what is the problem at Keefer Hall? Is it the Cavalier, Knagg, acting up?'

Every field of endeavor has its stars. Diamond lovers have the tragic legend of the Koh-i-noor at their fingertips. Members of the turf have the Goldolphin Barb, the Byerley Turk, and the Darley Arabian. For those who delve into the spirit world, the stars were Longleat's Green Lady and Knagg, the ghostly Cavalier of Keefer Hall.

'I think not,' he said, frowning over the letter. 'It seems to be a new ghost, not the famous Cavalier or the singing nun we read so much about. I shall be happy to look into it and settle the ghost down for the countess, if possible.' That modest 'if possible' was purely a matter of form. When Mr Wainwright dealt with ghosts, he came out the victor.

He did not claim to be an exorcist or anything of that sort. Merely he was attuned to hauntings. He could walk into a room and tell the owner exactly who or what it was that was banging doors or moaning in the night or peeping out from dark corners to frighten the inhabitants out of their wits. He appeared to have the power to commune with these spirits and discover their complaints. His method was to treat them as if they were still living, to discuss matters rationally with them. After all,

3

they had been people once; their nature did not change because the body had passed on to another level of existence. He always managed to placate the haunting spirits.

Charity had been surprised to discover how often the owner was on good terms with his ghost. Folks usually did not want to be rid of the haunting but merely to discover the who and why of it. Charity did not share her papa's unusual power, had never seen any ghosts. In fact, some secret part of her heart doubted their very existence in spite of some of the strange things she had witnessed when working with her papa. But she never for a moment doubted that he believed in these spirits. His whole life revolved around them. He was a founding member of the Society for the Study of Discarnate Beings. When he was not visiting a house to search for spirits, he was toiling over dusty tomes and tracts, tracing this phenomenon to its ancient roots. He was familiar with the history of all of the famous ghosts of England and was on a first-name basis with many of them.

This vast wealth of knowledge certainly impressed the clients who called on him. 'Old Tom is acting up, is he?' he had remarked calmly to Lady John Mulliner as he was shown into her saloon last year.

'Why, how did you know Tom's name? And how did you know he has become so terribly restless?' his hostess had demanded.

4

Charity had seen her papa reading up on Tom, the ghostly gardener of Englemere, before he left home. Tom had been shot through the heart in 1763 when he was caught trifling with the daughter of the house. Why would Lady John have called for Papa at this particular time if Tom had not been disturbing her?

'I had a feeling in my bones,' Papa had said modestly.

At such times Charity felt her papa was a fraud. Yet there had been other occasions when she was forced to consider the possibility that he actually did possess some power. He ofttimes knew things about ghosts that he had never been told of or read about. Subsequent investigations into the records of the house confirmed his theories.

Charity had been with him at St Martin's Priory when he had walked into the attic and said, 'A young woman—unhappy over a love affair. She was locked up in here, but she did not die in this room.'

'That is right!' Sir Harold Morton had exclaimed. 'By Jove, Wainwright, you did not read *that* anywhere, for I only discovered it myself last month. Miss Harley was poisoned in her bedchamber. She left a diary hidden under the floorboards here in the attic. It was after I removed it that the walking and moaning began. The chamber is right above our bedroom, you must know. It bothers my

5

wife.'

'There were some letters as well,' Papa had said.

'Yes! Yes, there was a little packet of six letters. My wife has them put away somewhere. They are quite valuable.'

'It is the letters your spirit wishes returned, Sir Harold. They are from her lover. The presence is weak. It must be very old. Late seventeenth century, I think?'

'The letters are dated 1690.'

'Put back the letters and the lady will soon depart. I shall ask her to leave the letters. Ghosts do not last forever. Eventually they must be getting on with the work of eternity.'

Sir Harold returned the letters and the ghost was heard of no more. The letters were left behind.

'You are sure Lord Merton approves of your visit?' Charity asked. She knew from experience that an inhospitable host could make a visit unpleasant.

'Why would he not? "A most troublesome affair," his mama calls it. She urges me to come as soon as possible. Very likely they have discommoded a spirit in some manner. Having renovations done, for instance, will often set a spirit off.'

'Where is Keefer Hall, exactly?' Charity asked, wondering if it would be a long trip.

'It is in Hampshire, only sixty miles away. Eastleigh is the closest village, two or three

6

miles this side of Keefer Hall. If we leave tomorrow morning, we can be in Eastleigh in time for dinner at a local inn and arrive at Keefer Hall in the evening to tour the Hall.'

His daughter did not mention that as Keefer Hall was so close they might continue on and have dinner there. Papa did not like such a tame opening act for his performance. He would have scowled to hear her use the word *performance*, but over the years a theatrical quality had crept into his work. He would arrive in his black carriage, which bore the crest of the Society for the Study of Discarnate Beings in a small lozenge on the doors, like a nobleman's crest. The carriage was drawn by four matching black horses.

Mr Wainwright would be wearing black evening clothes, with a black cape lined in white satin swirling behind him. He used his silver-headed walking stick with all the flair of a magician about to perform some feat of legerdemain. He liked to hear a gasp of disbelief when he pointed the silver knob and announced, 'Here! This is where the spirit emanates from. You have an angry ghost, milady. A victim of murder!'

Charity did not have to be told that the optimum hours for ghost hunting were between eleven p.m. and two a.m. She also knew that she must pack proper gowns for evening wear. Her papa did not accept money for his work. He went as a guest, always accompanied by his daughter. Mary wished it so, and one could hardly deny a ghost such a simple request. Mary was Wainwright's late wife. It was her untimely passing ten years before that had set him off on his passion for the supernatural. Unable to bear his grief, he had visited a medium, who had succeeded in calling up Mary's presence, or so he believed.

Within six months he had given up his seat in Parliament and gone into ghost hunting full time. A year later he had changed his team of bays for the black team and had his tailor fashion the satin-lined cape. As a younger son, Wainwright did not have an estate to hamper him. He had a home in London and a competence that made working for a living unnecessary, so with his special aptitude he had given his life over to this strange hobby.

That evening Charity looked up the Mertons in the *Peerage of England, Scotland and Ireland*. She discovered that Keefer Hall was owned by the Dechastelaines. Besides the Countess of Merton (née Lady Anne Carstairs), there was her son John (Earl of Merton) and his younger brother Lewis (Viscount Winton). A little arithmetic told her that the sons were thirty and nineteen years of age, respectively. No wives were mentioned. This being the case, she took considerable pains to pack her best gowns.

'Will I need my riding habit, Papa?' she asked before packing it.

'Not this time, my dear. But you should pack your new evening frock. There will be a party of some sort.'

Charity did not question this. Papa seemed to know these things. His knowledge did not come from his hostesses' letters, but from that infinite beyond with which he was in communication. He had other occult powers as well as being a ghost hunter. She left out the riding habit but was happy to hear that she would be attending an assembly or a ball.

As she spent too little time in London to nab a *parti* there, she had decided to cast her net in whatever waters her papa's work took her to. Although not an Incomparable, Miss Wainwright was by no means an antidote. Her brown hair curled naturally about her heart-shaped face. Her figure was lithe, her nose was straight, her teeth were white, and her eyes were blue. Added to these respectable claims to beauty, she had a gracious manner, smoothed by years of mixing with society. Several promising beaux had been lost due to a hasty dart to quell some new ghost. Papa was too good at his work. He settled the ghost problem before Charity reached a settlement with a young man.

They left the next morning for Keefer Hall.

*   *   *

It was while awaiting their arrival that

afternoon that Lady Merton admitted to having invited the Wainwrights. She sat in the elegant Blue Saloon with her two sons. Lewis, Viscount Winton, had recently been sent down from Cambridge for having written a lewd translation of some lines from Juvenal's *Satires*. As it was the third time the university had deemed it necessary to remove his corrupting influence from its halls, he had high hopes that he would not have to return.

The regimen of occasionally having to read a book other than poetry and discuss it with a tutor was anathema to the young viscount. His soul craved romance and found the closest thing to it in aping his idol, Lord Byron.

'What, you have invited that old quack who thinks he talks to ghosts?' Lord Merton exclaimed in disgust.

'He is not a quack, John,' Lady Merton replied. 'Far from it. Lady Montagu gave an excellent account of his powers.'

'Lady Montagu is a scatterbrained, idle lady with nothing better to do than imagine she is seeing ghosts.'

'It is as well known as an old ballad that Beaulieu has a brown monk who haunts it. Everyone has seen it.'

'*I* have not seen it, and I have been there a dozen times,' Merton replied.

'You never see anything,' his mama retaliated.

'By the living jingo,' Lord Winton

10

exclaimed, 'a ghost hunter! That will be something like. We will get a look at Knagg at last.' Then he remembered his role and assumed a sneer as he turned to Merton. 'Open up your soul to this opportunity, John. There are more things in heaven and earth than ... than ...' he floundered to a halt. He was not so keen on Shakespeare as on Byron.

'Ass!' Merton said with a blighting stare. 'And, for God's sake, get rid of that ludicrous kerchief. You look like a racetrack tout.'

There was little resemblance between the mother and her sons. The lady was a petite blonde, a vaporish woman in whom beauty was beginning to dwindle to petulance. The latter were both tall and dark. Lewis was the more handsome. At nineteen, his most outstanding feature was his large and lustrous blue eyes that glowed with dreams of resplendent glory and romance. A glance at the older brother suggested how he would look in another decade, when time had deluded his boyish fancies, had strengthened his jaw and defined his nose to a more manly shape—and, it was hoped, had quelled the riotous excess of his toilette. The blue-and-white-dotted Belcher kerchief at his throat waged an aesthetic battle with a red-and-gold-striped waistcoat. Over the whole was a nip-waisted jacket by Stutz that sported brass buttons as big as saucers. It was only his youth and excellent physique that saved him from looking a perfect quiz.

No one had ever accused Merton of dandyism. If his mama had a complaint, it was that he took too little interest in fashion. He spurned the stylish Brutus do that looked so good on Lewis and wore his short hair brushed back. His jackets, severely tailored with modest brass buttons, were of the best material and impeccably cut, but they did not aspire to the latest heights of fashion. She would have preferred his going off to London for the Season instead of staying at Keefer Hall to tend to his several thousand acres. Lord Merton chose to go to London in the dead of winter, when no one of any account was there, only dull politicians. Lewis would have preferred a Season as well, but since the ghost hunters were coming, he thought perhaps the summer would not be a total loss.

'I daresay the helmet has hit the floor again. Is that what is bothering you?' Merton asked his mama. It was Knagg's bothersome custom to play with the military effects in the Armaments Room.

'Why should *that* bother me?' she snapped. 'That has been going on forever.'

'The floor is uneven. I must see to it one of these days. If it is not Knagg, then what on earth has induced you to invite this Wainwright fellow?' Merton asked.

'I have told you *three times*, John, there is a ghost in my bedchamber. I have not had a good night's sleep for a month.'

12

'What you have, Mama, is a very old house, with floors that squeak and squawk and a chimney that howls when the wind is high.'

'It is not that! She comes to the window at night.'

'Close your curtains,' he said firmly.

'I *do* close them. She opens them. And she ... she appears from the clothespress as well,' Lady Merton said with an air of embarrassment.

Merton suppressed the phrase 'mad as a hatter.' Mama had been looking peaked of late. That she had recently replaced her dresser with a full-time companion, Miss Monteith, a former upstairs maid, suggested that she was either lonesome or frightened. She had been seeing a good deal of St John, the vicar, as well. Something was obviously bothering her. Of course she was reaching that age ... If it amused her to have a ghost hunter, there was no real harm in it. He would tip the fellow the clue that he must be rid of the ghost at top speed and give him ten guineas, and that would be the end of it.

'When does he come?' he asked.

'He will be arriving this evening. Around eleven.'

'Eleven? That is a demmed uncivil hour to call.'

'You need not be here, John. I shall greet Mr Wainwright and his daughter and make them welcome.'

13

'Good God! Does he travel with his whole family?'

'Only one daughter.'

'Daughter?' Lewis asked, his eyes shining.

'Miss Wainwright is his amanuensis,' Lady Merton explained. 'She keeps notes of his findings.'

'And scribbles them up to amuse the public.' Merton scowled. All the world would read of his mama's folly.

'Is she pretty?' Lewis asked.

'Lady Montagu said she is a good-natured creature.'

The gentlemen exchanged knowing looks. 'An antidote,' Merton translated. 'The ugly ones are always called good-natured.'

In theory, any lady who fell an inch short of perfection was of no interest to Lewis. In practice, he was a good deal less demanding. 'Pity,' he said. 'What age, Mama?'

Merton turned a fulminating eye on him. 'You are not to carry on with the chit, Lewis. That is all we need, you making an ass of yourself over that charlatan's daughter.'

'Damme, John, that is unfair. My interest in all this is purely literary. Look at the thundering success old Coleridge had with his ghostly wedding guest.'

'What the devil is he talking about?' Merton asked his mama.

'It is something about a bird, dear, an albatross, I believe, and water, water

14

everywhere, but strangely the sailors are all dying of thirst.'

'Ignorant as swans,' Lewis scoffed with a condemning look at his family. 'It is about sin, and expiation, and . . . and shrieving the soul. It is all an allegory, you see. The albatross is a symbol. I wonder if there is an allegory in Knagg. I shall speak to Mr Wainwright. It seems to me Knagg—'

'Do gag him, for God's sake,' Lady Merton said with an appealing look at her elder son.

'Put a damper on it. You are giving Mama the megrims.'

'Very well, I shan't bother you mental commoners with poetical things. But it will be jolly good sport hunting ghosts.'

Merton rose. 'We have work to do, Lewis. An estate of ten thousand acres does not run itself. It is time you learned the ropes. If you cannot profit from a higher education, then you must learn to farm, to be ready to take over your own place when you reach your maturity. I have enough to do with the Hall. In the spring I can use another pair of hands. Take a run over to the east meadow. Wallins is shearing the sheep today. See if he needs any of the fellows to help him. And you might see that the storage barn has been cleaned up to take the new wool. I shall be in my office.'

Lewis assumed a pained expression and quoted, '"Happy the man who . . . works his ancestral acres with oxen of his own breeding,"

15

eh, John? I envy you your simple pleasures.'

'You omitted the best part of Horace's lines. "Free from usury." And as you seem unaware of the fact, I might add it is *sheep* I breed, not oxen.'

'What is the difference? They are all smelly quadrupeds.'

'One does not shear oxen.'

Lewis was happy enough once he reached the outdoors. So long as he could perform his duties astride his mount, he had no real complaints. Even a poet needed a sound mind in a sound body. How was a fellow to keep a sound body if he was forever bent over a book? He took his gun with him, to hunt a few rabbits before dinner.

Lady Merton sat on alone, worrying. She knew John did not take her fears seriously, but they *were* genuine fears. Her past was enough to frighten anyone. And now her nemesis had come back to haunt her. She should never have done what she did to Meg. The vicar said this was her chance to undo her sins before she had to meet her maker. That was the way to look at it, as an opportunity to rectify the past.

CHAPTER TWO

The Wainwrights arrived in Eastleigh late in the afternoon, with plenty of time to make a reconnaissance trip to view the exterior of Keefer Hall. It was all that a ghost hunter could wish. In the distance a Gothic heap rose against a dull gray sky. Mr Wainwright gazed contentedly at pointed windows, finials, gargoyles, and a steeply canted roof.

'There are the ravens,' he said, pointing to six bumps on the roof line. 'At Longleat the departure of the swans will foretell the end of the family line. Here at Keefer Hall there is a legend that the ravens circle the house to foretell good luck.'

The birds sat immobile as statues for as long as Charity looked at them. The surrounding park featured dank yews and dripping elms that cast long shadows on the grass. She feared the chimneys in such an old house would smoke; the rooms would be dark and dreary, and the inhabitants would discuss nothing but ghosts and gout.

'I shouldn't be surprised if they have an oubliette, complete with skeletons and clanking chains,' she said.

'Such appurtenances are not necessary to a haunting,' her papa replied. 'Though they do add a certain atmosphere, of course. We shall return to Eastleigh, have a stroll around the town to stretch our limbs, then hire a room to change into evening-wear. After dinner we shall return to Keefer Hall.'

At the inn after their stroll, Charity washed away the dust of travel and changed into her blue silk evening gown, trimmed with Belgian lace around the skirt and bodice. She would have preferred a lighter color in spring. The blue was not the blue of a summer sky, but a deep Wedgwood blue that matched her eyes. Papa liked her to look somber, to add to the atmosphere. She had put her foot down at wearing black, however. She was neither a witch nor a widow, after all.

Mr Wainwright was rigged out in his ghost-hunting outfit of black evening clothes, satin-lined cape, and silver-headed ebony walking stick. He cut quite a dash when the black carriage, pulled by four jet-black horses, thundered up to the door of Keefer Hall.

Lewis, who darted out to greet them, was immensely impressed. Now here was a gentleman with a sense of style! Wainwright brought a whiff of brimstone with him, with that swirling cape and those slashes of black eyebrow. The daughter was not the clumsy, snorting sort of female he had feared either. Quite pretty, actually, and a little older, just as he liked. She was in her early twenties, he judged, by no means hagged—and with a dandy figure. Wouldn't the fellows at Cambridge stare to hear he was intimate with an older lady!

'Welcome to Keefer Hall!' he said, ushering them in.

Wainwright introduced himself and his daughter. 'Lady Merton is expecting me, I

18

think,' he said.

'We are all waiting for you. If you would like to remove your cape...'

'I shall keep it, thank you. Ghosts bring a chilly air with them.'

'Ah!' Lewis grinned his approval of this bit of arcane lore. 'Come into the saloon and have a glass of something wet before we begin work.'

'Excellent! A glass of claret sharpens the senses. And there is no hurry. Midnight is the best hour for communing with the beyond.'

Lewis hung on his every word, already envisaging himself in a cape of similar design (though perhaps a red lining would be more dramatic), banishing ghosts from damsels' castles and taking his reward in the ladies' boudoirs. The Wainwrights were soon being introduced to an elegant, pretty, but troubled lady of middle years who was clutching a lace-edged handkerchief.

Wainwright bowed over her bejewelled fingers and said in a low voice, 'Fear not, Lady Merton, we shall clear up that past transgression that is troubling you. It was not entirely your fault.'

She gasped in wonder and said, 'I am *so* glad you are here, Mr Wainwright.'

Lord Merton heard her incredulous gasp and shot a narrow-eyed glance at the callers. He saw his mother staring fatuously at the man. What had the scoundrel said to Mama?

Charity saw his annoyance. Oh, dear! It was to be one of those visits, where the man of the house disapproved of them. She was at pains to distract him.

'What an interesting house, Lord Merton,' she said. 'The façade is very old, I think?' She was relieved to observe that the interior had been modernized. No smoke emanated from the blazing grate of an Adam fireplace. Fine mahogany furnishings gleamed from a recent application of beeswax and turpentine. A pair of striped sofas were arranged by the grate. Around them stretched a vast room, done up in a style suitable to a noble home.

Merton did the decent thing and behaved civilly to his mama's guests. 'Yes, the front and parts of the west wing survive from the fifteenth century. The place was pretty well destroyed by the Ironsides. We had Cromwell's troopers billeted here in the 1600s. The Dechastelaines were Royalists.'

'You are fortunate anything was left standing.'

'We have the restoration of Charles II to thank for that. Our so-called ghost, Knagg, was one of the Cavaliers who was killed here, defending Keefer Hall. In the Armaments Room we have a yellow jerkin and a helmet allegedly belonging to the fellow who killed him. I daresay it was Knagg's violent end that accounts for these ghost stories. That is what you folks hold to account for ghosts, is it not?'

20

'Violent or tragic,' she said, noticing but not commenting on his many evasions: 'so-called ghost,' 'allegedly,' 'I daresay,' 'what you folks hold to account.' All this told her that Lord Merton was not a believer. 'Papa will tell you the exact nature of his passing.'

Merton shot her a look not a shade short of outright derision.

Charity did not foam up in anger. It was not her way, but she did not back down either. 'I take it our invitation does not have your approval, milord?'

'If it amuses Mama...' The old fool Wainwright, rigged up like a satellite of Satan in a morality play, could say what he liked without fear of contradiction as there was no proof to counter his story. 'I personally place no credence in ghosts,' he said bluntly. 'I have lived at Keefer Hall for thirty years without seeing any spirits or hearing the singing nun.'

'Some are insensitive in that respect,' she replied, refusing to take offense, and immediately changed the subject. 'I assume there was a priory hereabouts at one time, as you speak of the ghost of a nun.'

'Yes, an offshoot of the monastery, as the priories usually were in the old days, I believe. Keefer Hall stands on the remains of an old Cistercian monastery. The cloisters still stand. The chapel, unfortunately, was looted by Cromwell. It is considered an excellent example of its sort. Whitewashed walls, the stained glass taken out, a plain black cross. We do not use it.'

Lewis was bored with this sort of chat. Just like John to go talking history when he had this rare opportunity to broaden his horizons with some *really* interesting conversation. 'Tell us some of your ghost experiences, Miss Wainwright. I find it fascinating,' he said.

'One hardly knows where to begin.' She wished Lord Winton had chosen some other subject as the master of the house was looking at her with a jaundiced eye, ready to poke holes in any claims she made. 'Monks and nuns appear in a greater proportion than their actual numbers warrant. The Society believes it was their harsh treatment by Henry VIII that accounts for it.'

'What society is that?' Lewis asked.

'The Society for the Study of Discarnate Beings,' she replied. 'Papa is a founding member of it.'

Merton snorted openly.

'How would a fellow go about joining it?' Lewis asked.

Merton said, 'Let us hope the society's rules are more lenient than Cambridge's or you will not last long.'

Charity looked a question at him. Before either could speak, Lewis cleared his throat and said, 'We shall speak of it another time. Do you ride, Miss Wainwright?'

'Yes, indeed, but I did not bring my riding

22

habit.'

'Daresay Mama may have one to fit you.'

As his mama was six inches shorter and the same measure wider than Miss Wainwright, she stared to hear this.

'Don't be an ass, Lewis,' his brother said. 'In any event, the Wainwrights will soon find our ghosts and leave. They are not here to ride—or to shanghai members for Mr Wainwright's ghost society.'

Charity knew how to handle the brusque manner of a nonbeliever. 'Just so,' she said demurely. 'Actually, membership is severely restricted. There is a waiting list of over a hundred applicants.'

They finished their claret and Mr Wainwright rose. 'Let the hunting begin,' he announced in dramatic accents.

'I shall accompany you!' Lewis said, jumping up at once.

Lady Merton also rose and began to lead the way. Lord Merton stood, looking after them with an expression not much short of a sneer on his chiseled face. He did not move as the party walked to the door. Charity looked over her shoulder, not an invitation but merely a curious look. Merton's cool glance measured her lithe form and the nest of curls atop her head. The eyes were rather good ... It might be amusing to see how that *poseur* of a Wainwright conned the ladies. He set down his glass and followed the little group into the hallway. Lewis put a possessive hand on Charity's elbow and began to ask her how he should apply for membership in the Society.

At the foot of the stairs Mr Wainwright stopped. His body assumed the rigid posture of a pointer on the scent of its quarry. He lifted his silver-knobbed cane in a dramatic gesture and pointed it down the hall. His satin-lined cape swirled with the motion of his arm.

'A very strong presence in that direction. A young male—angry about something. Can you not feel the cold blast?'

'I feel it! A regular Arctic blast,' Lewis said. Charity had intimated a sensitivity to spirits was highly regarded in the Society.

'That is where Knagg lives, in the Armaments Room!' Lady Merton exclaimed. 'Fancy your feeling him from this far away, Mr Wainwright.'

Merton's gaze turned to the doorway, where a breeze stiff enough to ruffle a muffler Lewis had tossed on a chair blew in from the ill-fitting door.

'I must have that door rehung,' he murmured.

Lady Merton led the party up the grand staircase to her bedchamber. At the top of the stairs Wainwright again stopped, listened, raised his silver-knobbed cane, and this time pointed it west. 'A young woman,' he said. 'It is an affair of the heart.'

Lady Merton gasped, then frowned. 'But my

bedchamber with the ghost is to the east, Mr Wainwright.'

Lord Merton pinched his lips between his teeth to squelch his laugh of triumph. He cast a quick glance at Miss Wainwright, who smiled softly, undismayed and unoffended.

'If Papa says there is a female ghost in the west wing, milord, you will find there is such a specter there,' she said.

Lewis was unhappy to lose Miss Wainwright's attention. 'John could not find an elephant in a closet, where ghosts are concerned,' he said.

'Odd this specter has never troubled me. I sleep in the west wing,' Merton replied.

'I have seen her a dozen times,' Lewis said. 'A gray lady slipping along the corridor.'

'Miss Monteith, no doubt,' his brother replied. 'Shall we continue on to Mama's room—despite Mr Wainwright's having failed to sense any disturbance there?'

'Indeed. We shall return to the young lady and Knagg anon,' Wainwright agreed, and they continued eastward.

Charity, knowing she would not sense any ghostly apparition, looked at Lady Merton's bedchamber with a clear eye. She saw an extremely elegant room with handpainted wallpaper featuring bluebirds and roses. The same pattern appeared on the creamy carpet. The furnishings were dainty French pieces, the chaise lounge upholstered in the same shade of blue as the birds on the walls. On a table beside it rested a decanter of wine and a novel. A blue lustring bed canopy and pelmetted window drapes added a little too much blue to the chamber to please her, although it was elegant. The toilet table boasted a host of cosmetic bottles, their chased silver lids matching the dresser set. The air was heavy with the cloying scent from two large bouquets of pink roses.

Wainwright looked around, frowning. He went to the suspect window, glanced out, shook his head, and turned to the clothespress. He opened the door, looked in, then shook his head again. 'You have no ghost here, milady.'

Lady Merton's pretty face puckered in annoyance. 'Nonsense! I know a ghost when I see one. She came right out of that clothespress two nights ago,' she said, pointing to it. 'Sometimes she comes to my window.'

Wainwright smiled condescendingly. 'As you have experienced these apparitions, then I can only assume your ghost has left. They *do* leave eventually, you must know—though it is strange there should be no lingering trace so soon after an apparition. They usually dwindle, becoming weaker, finally leaving entirely. I sense no trace whatsoever here.'

'Try my sitting room,' she said, and led the way into it. 'Oh, you are here, Miss Monteith!' she exclaimed.

A tall, angular female of middle years rose at their entrance and regarded them with a saurian eye. Her graying hair was bound tightly and covered with a cap. Her plain dove-gray gown suggested she was a higher class of servant.

'I was just fixing the hem on your skirt, milady,' she said with a brief curtsy.

'This is my companion, Miss Monteith,' Lady Merton said. 'This is the gentleman I have invited to look into the ghost, Miss Monteith. And his daughter, Miss Wainwright.'

While the introduction was being acknowledged, Mr Wainwright stared hard at Miss Monteith. He said nothing, but as soon as they left, he said to Lady Merton, 'How long has that woman been with you?'

'Why, forever. She was here when I married Lord Merton thirty-five years ago.'

'Ah. I had thought her arrival to be of more recent date. I would advise you to get rid of her. She is not good for you.'

'I could not do that!' Lady Merton exclaimed. 'Miss Monteith is an old and trusted servant.'

'Banish her to some other part of the house at least.'

'You are on the wrong track, Mr Wainwright,' Lady Merton said stiffly. 'I invited you to find my ghost and help me be rid of her, not to rearrange my household.'

Lord Merton liked the notion of getting rid of Miss Monteith. He noticed his mama was always disturbed after being closeted with the woman. As he hoped Wainwright might yet prove helpful, he said in a pleasant way, 'Shall we go along and visit Knagg now?'

'Go ahead,' Lady Merton said. 'I shall retire. Thank you for coming, Mr Wainwright. It was kind of you to undertake the trip.' She moved a step closer and added in a lowered voice, 'We shall speak again tomorrow about ... what you said earlier.'

'Indeed we shall.' He bowed ceremoniously and left.

The group did not proceed immediately to visit Knagg.

'While we are above stairs, I must have just a little look at that west corridor where the emanation is so strong,' Wainwright said.

Merton pinched his lips together and led the way. When they were halfway down the corridor, Wainwright stopped. 'Yes, the presence is overwhelming here. Can you not feel the bone-chilling wind?' He drew his cape around him, flinging one corner over his shoulder in a manner to reveal its satin lining.

'No, I cannot say that I do,' Merton replied.

Charity was uncertain. It was chillier, but as they had just left Lady Merton's room, where the grate was blazing, that might account for it.

'I am frozen to the marrow,' Lewis said, turning up his collar.

'This is the old part of the house,' Merton explained. 'Odd you mention a female presence, sir.'

'A nun. Definitely a young nun,' Wainwright said.

A triumphant smile seized Merton's face. 'I am afraid you are mistaken. The nuns were housed in the priory, a mile to the west. They were never allowed here. This is where the monks slept.'

'She was killed in that room,' Wainwright said, pointing his silver knob at the door. 'May I enter, Lord Merton?'

'That is my bedchamber! I assure you there are no ghosts in there.'

'What are you afraid of, John?' Lewis taunted.

Wainwright said nothing, but he gave him such an imperative look that Merton opened the door. 'She was murdered just there,' he said, pointing to the fireplace.

'Burned alive!' Lewis exclaimed. 'Immolated in flames, like Joan of Arc.'

'No, shot right here,' Wainwright said, placing his hand on his chest.

'But that is certainly the singing nun!' Lewis said. 'She is reported as having a dark stain on the bodice of her habit. Odd it was done in the grate.'

'The house has obviously undergone renovations,' Wainwright explained.

'That is true,' Merton said grudgingly. 'I have just told you there were rows of monks' cells along this corridor at one time. When it was rebuilt, naturally that was changed. We are not monks after all.'

Wainwright said, 'We shall learn more anon. Now let us proceed to Knagg. I cannot tell you how long I have wanted to get into Keefer Hall, milord. Very kind of you to invite me.'

'It was Mama who invited you. I daresay you have been studying the literature of Keefer Hall, Mr Wainwright?'

Charity saw what he was getting at and resented it. He was trying to show Papa up as a fraud.

'I am pretty familiar with all the literature and legends of our English ghosts,' Wainwright admitted. 'But the literature does not mention the nun being in that particular area. She is said to haunt the cloisters.'

'So folks say,' Merton agreed. One thing he did approve of was Wainwright's cautioning his mama against Miss Monteith. He mentioned this to his guest. 'I cannot believe the woman is good for her.'

'She is bent on mischief. I would not let her within the walls of the house, but that is your affair. I only advise.'

'You sensed no ghost in Mama's rooms?' Lewis asked. 'I mean to say, you were not shamming it, to ease her mind?'

'I never sham it, Lord Winton. There is no ghost there.'

'Well, there is certainly one in the Armaments Room.'

Merton led the way down to this ancient timbered room, which had been lit in anticipation of the visit. It was hung with all manner of sword and halberd, ancient gun, spiked mace and pistol, helmet and bloodied flag, and even one small cannon. Suits of armor stood around the edge of the room, reminding Charity of a ball to which too many gentlemen had been invited.

'Ah!' Wainwright sighed blissfully. 'Yes, indeed! The place is alive with spirits. You have not one ghost here, milord, but at least two. Both young men. One Cavalier—that would be Knagg—and one of Cromwell's Ironsides. They are at daggers drawn over—that!' he said, pointing to a table to the left of the grate.

They all went forward to examine the cause of the mischief. A yellow jerkin and a round helmet sat on a table, along with an assortment of old pistols.

'Now that is odd!' Lewis said. 'The servants complain of finding the little yellow jacket and the helmet on the floor a dozen times a month.'

Wainwright explained, 'The Royalist ghost does not want it on that table. He would prefer to have those reminders of Cromwell out of the room entirely or at least not on display.'

'They are a part of the history of Keefer Hall,' Merton said. 'I could not allow them to be removed.'

'At least move them to a separate table,' Wainwright said. 'You will have no peace until

31

you do.'

Lewis closed his eyes and said, 'I get a sense that Knagg is sore that Cromwell's relics are mixed up with the Royalist ones.' From beneath his eyelids he peered at Wainwright for confirmation.

'That is the obvious answer,' Wainwright agreed. 'Common sense comes into it, too.'

'I am surprised to hear it,' Merton said.

'Let us not move them yet,' Wainwright continued. 'It might make the ghosts depart, and I would like a word with them before that happens.'

Merton looked at him, astonishment elevated to irony. 'You need not fear I intend to change anything in my house to suit a ghost, Mr Wainwright. And now that you have met all the spectral guests of Keefer Hall, perhaps you would like a bite of meat before retiring.'

'I shall join you in the saloon shortly, milord. I would just like a word with Charles.'

Lewis said, 'Eh? Our butler's name is Bagot.'

'I refer to your Parliamentary ghost and his friend, the Cavalier. They are related—by blood, I mean. Brothers or stepbrothers or cousins. Not brothers-in-law. It is sad to have families at odds. I shall try to arrange a reconciliation.'

Lewis weighed Charity's charms against her papa's and opted for the latter. 'I shall stay and give you a hand, sir.'

'Good luck,' Merton said. He offered his

32

arm to Charity and said, 'Would you care to join me in the Blue Saloon, ma'am? There is a matter I should like to discuss with you.'

She felt a quiver of apprehension. Surely he was not going to ask them to leave! That would be a new low in Papa's career. And Lady Merton would not come to their rescue as Papa had not found a ghost in her bedchamber. She knew perfectly well that Merton thought her papa a fraud, so he could not want to discuss ghosts. But no, they would not be leaving yet. Papa had told her to bring her new evening frock and he was seldom mistaken about such things.

CHAPTER THREE

The servants were preparing tea when Charity and Lord Merton entered the Blue Saloon. Two young girls were placing a large silver tray that held the tea set, dishes, sandwiches, and a plate of sweets on the sofa table before the grate. Merton spoke idly of inconsequential matters until they had left, inquiring if Miss Wainwright had had a pleasant trip and such things.

As soon as the servants disappeared, his polite smile faded and he said frankly, 'Miss Wainwright, I have made no secret of the fact that I think this visit an exercise in futility. That is not to say, however, that I fail to realize something is bothering Mama. She has not been herself lately. I hope that you and your papa can assist her.'

'We shall do what we can, milord,' she replied, with more curiosity than offense. 'How do you think we can be of help if her problem is not of a supernatural order?'

He batted his hand impatiently. 'There is no such thing as a supernatural order—barring religion, I mean,' he added.

'Because you have not observed any supernatural phenomena does not necessarily mean they do not exist,' she pointed out politely.

'No sane person has observed anything of the sort. It is nonsense. Ghosts and goblins are creatures of the imagination to frighten children and the ignorant, superstitious lower orders.'

'The Society for the Study of Discarnate Beings numbers several gentlemen of no mean intellectual accomplishments. We have a professor from Oxford and an elderly gentleman who is a retired bishop.'

'A senile, superannuated clergyman might well be prey to imaginings.'

'The Oxford professor is only fifty years old. How can you be so certain *you* are right and the rest of us are wrong? Your own mama and Lord Winton believe.'

'Mama is in a highly nervous condition. She

34

is obviously hallucinating. As to Lewis!'

'Half the nobility of England believe in ghosts,' she said. 'You may believe or not, but you are in no position to call it all nonsense.'

He pinned her with a gimlet glance and demanded, 'Have *you* ever seen a ghost?'

'No. I have never seen the world looking anything but flat either, but I believe it is round.'

'You are confusing science and superstition here, ma'am.'

'Science is superstition until it is proven otherwise! You forget Galileo was tried as a heretic and spent eight years in prison.'

Merton frowned in perplexity. He had not expected such a hard argument from a young lady, and a foolish one who believed in ghosts at that.

'Show me a ghost and I will be as keen a believer as the next man,' he said.

'We might just do that. Stranger things have happened. It is narrowminded of you to assume that because you do not understand something, it does not exist. Look at electricity! What a strange and wonderful thing it is. All that invisible energy stored up in the air.'

'I did not invite you here to convert me.'

'You have made it amply clear that you did not invite us at all.'

'I meant into the saloon, just now. I want to discuss Mama's predicament in a rational manner. Personally, I think this harping on ghosts and such things can only harm her, in her delicate mental condition.'

'A festering mental wound does not heal itself by being covered up, though, any more than a physical one does. It must be treated, the poison let out.'

'Just so.' He leaned forward, eagerness lending a gleam to his dark eyes. 'Mama's particular aberration is that some ghost is harassing her. The logical cure is to be rid of the ghost.'

'That is why my father is here,' she replied in confusion.

'Yes, well, that is fine, but as I said, I do not believe in ghosts. As Mama does, however, the simplest cure would be to remove the ghost, would it not?'

'My father is not an exorcist, milord. You do not ease a mental strain by pretending it has gone away. If Lady Merton is troubled, you must discover the cause and treat it. Do you have any notion what is plaguing her?'

He gave a frustrated shake of his head. 'None in the least. She was perfectly normal until a month or so ago, when she began to complain of not being able to sleep. She seemed frightened of something. That is when she elevated Miss Monteith to her companion. I hoped that might be the end of Mama's megrims. I am sorry to say it, things have only got worse.'

'I see.' When Merton said nothing more, Charity continued. 'When Papa mentioned a young woman, and an affair of the heart, your mama became excited. I believe that described her ghost...' Merton gave a frown of impatience. 'Or what we shall call her ghost.'

'There is no young woman in the house except servants.'

'As your mama believes the woman to be a ghost, then the woman is obviously dead. She was speaking of the past. Some woman she associated with in her own youth, perhaps. It is odd Papa did not say a young *lady*,' she said, frowning.

As Miss Wainwright seemed a sensible person, barring this aberration of believing in ghosts, Merton wasted no more time, but plunged on to his specific request. 'I would like your father to get rid of this so-called ghost. How quickly do you think he can accomplish it?'

'That must depend on the circumstances, but he works quickly. I can say with reasonable certainty that the ghost will either be gone or will have stopped harassing your mama within a week.'

'Could he not do it more quickly—for a generous consideration, of course. I would be willing to pay—'

To Merton's astonishment, Miss Wainwright flew into the boughs. A thundercloud formed on her usually calm

37

countenance, and when she spoke, her voice was raised in anger.

'Lord Merton! Papa does not accept money! And to suggest a bribe! It is an insult. He feels he has certain powers that he shares with others as a favor, out of the kindness of his heart. It is a great imposition on his time—and mine—to be forever darting about the countryside.'

'I would not call it a bribe,' he said apologetically.

'I do not see what else you could call it. If you are implying that he should lie to Lady Merton, tell her the ghost has gone when it has not, I pray you will not mention anything of the sort to Papa. He would be grievously insulted at such a slur on his integrity.'

Merton felt extremely foolish. He had assumed that Wainwright, with his black carriage and team and his swirling cape, was a cunning fraud, who rid homes of their ghosts for a living. As this was not the case, he was left with nothing to say. His pride disliked to utter an apology. The only recourse was to attempt to rationalize his suggestion.

'It seems highly unlikely he will be able to come to terms with a ghost he cannot even find. He found no trace of Mama's ghost in her room. I feel it is a matter of some urgency to rid her mind of this unhealthy morass that possesses it.'

Charity gave him a rebukeful look but

considered his suggestion. 'If you really want to help her, you should discover what is causing her agitation. Perhaps it is not a ghost,' she allowed. 'People can have delusions about ghosts, as they can about anything else. That is not to say ghosts do not exist,' she added sharply. 'Only that they can be imagined to be where they are not. Though it is odd that she says she actually *saw* the ghost in her room on more than one occasion. When it is a delusion, it is usually more vague. A lurking shadow that pops up here and there, you know.'

'It is possible someone is creating this ghost to frighten her,' Merton said, and watched closely for Miss Wainwright's reaction. As she did not fly at him, he continued, 'It would be easily enough done. It comes to her window. A stuffed gown with a padded head hung on a rope from the roof...'

'I noticed the roof of Keefer Hall is sharply canted, though. One would have to be extremely agile to attempt anything of the sort. Could it possibly be the ravens she is mistaking for ghosts?'

'I hardly think so. She is perfectly familiar with them. They have been here forever. The "ghost" could be lowered from the window of the room above. There are attics and servants' quarters above the bedrooms. I cannot recall offhand just what is above Mama's room. I shall look into it in the morning.'

'What of the ghost that comes out of her

clothespress? It would be hard for someone to hide in there. The last thing her dresser would do at night would be to hang up her gown. She would see if someone was hiding there.'

'Miss Monteith is presently filling the role of dresser as well,' he said with a sapient look.

'You think Miss Monteith might be in on this masquerade?'

'I am not accusing her, but yes, I am suggesting it is possible. Particularly as the so-called haunting began around the time Miss Monteith became Mama's companion.'

Charity thought about this and said, 'My father is concerned only with legitimate ghosts. He does not investigate skulduggery of that sort. I would not leap to the conclusion that a ghost is not involved, despite your not believing. The Society is looking into the possibility that electricity is involved in some manner,' she added vaguely. 'Sometimes we must just accept what we cannot understand. A "willing suspension of disbelief," as our romantic poets describe it.'

'That is fine—for fiction, ma'am. I prefer good solid facts. I will suspend my disbelief when Mr Wainwright shows me hard evidence of a ghost. Meanwhile, I shall look into the more likely explanation that someone is frightening Mama.'

'That is your privilege,' she agreed blandly. 'Have you any idea why anyone would do such a thing? Does she have enemies?'

40

'None in the world, so far as I know. She lives a retired life here in the country. The mischief must be executed by someone within the house. Yet the servants like her...'

'Her reaction to Papa's mention of a young woman suggests to me that the root of her problem lies deep in the past. You should ask her about that.'

'If she has held her secret for thirty-odd years, it is not likely she will tell me about it now, is it?'

'No, for it must be something she is ashamed of.' Merton gave her a gimlet glance at this suggestion. 'No one has led a totally blameless life,' she added. 'Whether she is haunted by a ghost or only a feeling of guilt for some past transgression, her cure lies in righting that past wrong. Perhaps she will tell me. I am an outsider; I mean nothing to her. People will sometimes tell their secrets to a stranger when they will not tell their nearest and dearest.'

'I wish you would try to ingratiate yourself,' he said eagerly. 'If she could be weaned from Miss Monteith, that alone would be a step in the right direction.' His frown lightened and a small incipient smile moved his lips. 'She might very well talk to you, Miss Wainwright. I had no intention of opening my budget to you, and here I am, burdening you with our family problems—to say nothing of arguing with a guest. It was farouche of me.'

'Oh, I always enjoy a good argument with a

41

nonbeliever. I would be happy to help,' she replied. 'I sometimes feel *de trop* on these visits of Papa's. He has his ghost hunting; I am left at loose ends, with only a little note-taking to occupy my time.'

Merton studied her closely and liked what he saw. He was not a man to amuse himself with idle flirtations. He was known to have had a few mistresses in his time, and he kept an eye cocked for a suitable wife, but a conversable lady who was a friend was something new to him. He felt Miss Wainwright would be a comfortable friend. She did not flirt or behave in any manner that suggested a personal interest in him or his title or estate. She was quick to contradict him and argue; he liked that independence of spirit.

'As time hangs heavy on your hands, perhaps you would help me look into the nonghostly possibilities?' he said.

Charity recognized it as a bid for friendship and was happy to agree.

'We shall begin investigating the attic above Mama's room tomorrow morning. And have a look at the clothespress as well. But I must not abuse you with an excess of labor, as you are a guest, ma'am. We have an excellent stable at Keefer Hall.'

'I did not bring my riding habit.' Was it possible Papa had made a mistake?

'I recall now that Lewis already mentioned it.' He gave her a laughing look. 'Pity. I shan't suggest you wear Mama's, but could you not send home for your own?'

Charity thought about it for a moment, then said, 'I could, if you think we will not have worn out our welcome within two days. It would take a day to get the message to London and another day for the habit to arrive. I had the distinct impression you wished us at Jericho, milord.'

'Then I have been a very poor host. I pray you will forgive me. Like yourself, I have a sad tendency to say what I mean—which no doubt accounts for my lackluster performance in the Upper House. I will not say your papa is a fraud, but I think he is wasting his time. That is not to say we need waste ours. Send for the habit. In fact, I can send off a mounted footman and have it here by tomorrow evening. We shall ride the next day, if the weather is good.'

This eagerness from a handsome young lord caused a light flush of pleasure to suffuse Charity's cheeks. It was the only trace of the excitement that had invaded her being.

'That will be delightful,' she said. Then she added thoughtfully, 'But I daresay we will not ride. Papa told me I would not need my habit and he is never—well, seldom—wrong.'

Before Merton was required to acknowledge this troublesome speech, Lewis's heavy tread and fluting voice were heard in the hallway.

'By gad, Mr Wainwright, I never saw

anything like it.' Lewis and Wainwright duly appeared in the saloon and sat down for tea. As there was no hostess, Charity poured and Merton passed the sandwiches.

'Any luck in the Armaments Room, Mr Wainwright?' Merton asked politely.

Lewis answered for him. 'It was amazing, John. The helmet moved across the table of its own accord and fell to the floor while we were looking at it. And don't bother saying the table legs are crooked or the floorboards are slanted, for they ain't. I ran up to the nursery and brought down some marbles. Put 'em on the table and they didn't budge an inch. The table is flat all around. Nossir, it was Knagg pushing it off. Mr Wainwright is going to have it out with the pair of them while he is here—the Cavalier and Cromwell's Ironside. See if he can bring 'em together.'

Wainwright swelled with joy at this recital of his powers. To Merton he said, 'As to your mama's ghost, milord, I fear it is nothing of the sort. Something is pestering the poor soul, but it is not a ghost. Perhaps if she had a word with her vicar...'

His mama had already had too many words with the vicar to suit Merton. He felt that Monteith and the vicar between them were half her problem.

'Pity,' he said, 'but as you are here, you must by all means bring our other ghosts to heel, if possible.'

44

'Aye, the young lady in your bedroom interests me considerably.'

Merton's lips twitched, but he refrained from any of the outré remarks that occurred to him. It was for Lewis to shame the family.

'I shouldn't mind having a young lady in my bedchamber, Mr Wainwright. If John wants to be rid of her, you can send her to me.'

'That might be the quickest way to be rid of her,' Merton said with a blighting stare.

Wainwright quizzed Merton about the ghost in his room. When he had been assured a few times that Merton had never felt or seen any manifestation of the lady, he asked about the historical records of the house and was told that he must make himself free of the library.

When tea was finished, it was approaching one o'clock, and they all retired.

'Mama has given you Queen Elizabeth's bedchamber, Miss Wainwright,' Merton said with the air of one conferring an honor.

'How nice,' she said weakly.

Charity had slept in many lumpy beds formerly occupied by Queen Elizabeth, enough to make her wonder if the ancient queen had ever slept in her own bed. She was happy to see that at Keefer Hall the mattress was of more recent vintage than the sixteenth century. Accustomed to travel, she slept well. No echo of Lady Merton's ghost came to disturb her slumber. She did not hear until morning that there had been another

45

apparition.

CHAPTER FOUR

Normally Lady Merton would bestir herself to take breakfast at the table when she had guests, but guests who arose at eight were too much for her, especially after a restless night. She took toast and cocoa at ten in her bed. At eight-thirty the gentlemen and Miss Wainwright were tucking into gammon and eggs in the breakfast room, each looking forward to the excitement of the day's doings. Wainwright excused himself immediately after breakfast and went to the library to begin looking into the history of the Hall.

'Shall we begin our investigations now, Miss Wainwright?' Merton asked.

Lewis, his kerchief tamed to a proper cravat and his gaudy.waistcoat to a plain one, jumped up. 'What is this? *Your* investigations? Since when did you believe in ghosts, John? You called Wainwright a quack!' Lewis cast a quick, apologetic glance at the young lady. 'This is a trick to be with Miss Wainwright.'

'Quiet, cawker! We are only going to check the attic.'

'Mr Wainwright did not mention any ghosts there,' Lewis said accusingly. 'You are just trying to get her alone.'

'Mama's ghost is a dummy hung on a string outside her window to frighten her,' Merton said curtly. 'We are going to look for evidence of it.'

'I shall come along with you,' Lewis said at once, with a jealous peep at Charity, who pretended not to notice.

Lewis was easily swayed to consider that his mama's problem had a purely human cause. 'By gad, it could easily be done. I daresay Monteith still has the dummy she used concealed up there.'

'You assume that Miss Monteith is behind it?' Charity asked.

'Don't see who else it could be. Unless it is Sabourin,' he added, frowning. 'She was none too happy when Mama retired her, John. I think Sabourin had a few good years left in her, though she was nudging seventy.'

'Miss Sabourin was Mama's dresser,' Merton explained to Charity. 'Mama is paying her an excellent pension. Sabourin was happy to retire. As she is residing with her daughter in Eastleigh, I fail to see how she could be behind this mischief.'

They took their bearings on the landing before mounting to the attic. 'No one occupies the room above Mama's,' Lewis said. 'It is stuffed full of lumber.'

'Let us have a look,' Merton said, and they went up a narrow, uncarpeted stairway to the attic, past servants' quarters to that part of the

47

area used for storage. The room above Lady Merton's was as Lewis had described it. Old trunks, chairs and tables with broken legs, sofas with the stuffing half out, and other such discarded items filled the room. It was possible to move between the lumber, however, and they went to the window.

'No footprints,' Lewis mentioned.

'How could there be, there is a carpet,' Charity pointed out. 'Odd there should be a carpet on this part of the attic floor. The rest of it is not carpeted.'

A long strip of worn carpet ran from the doorway to the window. 'This is the bit of carpet you had replaced in the library hallway,' Lewis said to his brother.

'It has been laid to muffle the sound of footfalls,' Merton said, glancing down at it. 'I call that *prima facie* evidence that we are on the right track. Let us have a look at the window.'

It raised easily and noiselessly. He ran his finger along the groove. It came away smeared with oil. He tried the next window; it was hard to move and had not been treated with the oil. 'Now to find the stuffed gown,' he said, and they began peering behind furniture and opening trunks.

Lewis had a dandy time, reliving his childhood. 'Look at this, John! My first long trousers!' he exclaimed, drawing them out of a trunk. A flurry of moths hovered around the trousers. 'And here is my set of tin soldiers. I was wondering what had become of them.'

Before long he had assumed the role of Wellington, with his men arranged for battle, carefully positioned in the hills provided by folds of old clothing in the trunk. Whistling sounds of imaginary flying bullets punctuated the silence.

Charity looked at Merton and smiled.

'If he finds an officer's shako amidst this rubbish, he will have it on his head by lunchtime,' Merton said, and began looking around the room.

'There is nothing here,' he said after they had examined all possible hiding places. 'But I, for one, am certain this attic is the source of Mama's ghost. Why else was this one window oiled?'

'That still leaves the clothespress,' Charity said. She was a little disappointed that Merton had not mentioned sending off for her riding habit. It could hardly be at Keefer Hall by tomorrow if he waited much longer, yet she disliked to remind him of it.

'We shall leave Wellington here and get on with it,' he said, glancing at Lewis.

His brother was not that easily gotten rid of He stuffed the tin soldiers into his pockets and went below with them. In the hallway Merton said, 'This is Mama's room. Her sitting room is to the left and Miss Monteith's room is next to it. That does not give her access to the clothespress. It is in Mama's bedchamber, against the right-hand wall. The adjoining wall is in this room—a guest room,' he said, walking along and opening the door.

They went into a bright room done up in shades of gold and green. 'Mama's clothespress would be against this wall,' Merton said, walking hastily to the adjacent wall, where another clothespress stood. Merton was just about to open the door when Miss Monteith spoke from behind them. No one had heard her silent entry.

'Her ladyship would like to speak to you, Miss Wainwright,' she said. As she spoke, her eyes made a quick tour of the room. Her expression was not smiling, but it held a sort of secret irony.

Charity jumped in surprise. 'Oh, thank you, Miss Monteith. I did not hear you come in. I shall be happy to see her,' she said, and followed the woman out.

She found Lady Merton still in her bed, looking ten years older than she had looked the evening before. Her hair had been arranged and she wore a handsome silk bed jacket, but she had not applied her rouge.

'Miss Wainwright, kind of you to come.' She smiled sadly. 'I have been thinking about what your papa said last night, about there not being a ghost here.'

'He is quite certain there is no ghost in this part of the house, ma'am.'

'Yes, yes, I understand that. But you are a

woman—a lady—and you have considerable experience with this sort of thing as well. No doubt this power runs in families. I am not denying your father's powers, my dear. What he said to me last night the moment he came into the room convinces me he has great powers. But in this one case he has failed. The ghost came again last night. Not to the window, but from there,' she said, pointing to the clothespress.

'What did it look like?' Charity asked, glancing at Miss Monteith, who had taken up a stance behind Lady Merton and was listening with both ears.

'Oh, dear, it is difficult to say, in the dark, you know. She—the ghost, I mean—had opened the curtains again, letting in the moonlight. I made a particular point of closing them before going to bed. Miss Monteith will vouch for that.' Miss Monteith nodded firmly. 'By the light of the moon I saw a—how shall I say it?—disembodied spirit. A sort of smoke, or ether, coming from the clothespress. She had opened the clothespress door. I always make a point of closing it since ... recently.'

As the lady spoke of actually seeing the ghost, Charity did not like to suggest it did not exist. 'Who do you think it is?' she asked.

Lady Merton looked at Miss Monteith, who stared back, lizardlike. A secretive look came over Lady Merton's face. 'I am sixty years old, Miss Wainwright. No one has lived sixty years

51

without doing a little harm, however unintentional. It must be someone I have wronged in the past, do you not think?'

'That seems the likeliest answer,' Charity agreed. With Miss Monteith on the *qui vive*, she did not like to go into details. 'Perhaps if you could rectify this wrong, your ghost might leave.'

'Exactly what I thought. I am willing to do what I can to make restitution, and you must be rid of my ghost for me, for I cannot go on like this. She will be the death of me.'

When Charity looked at Miss Monteith again, the woman wore a very satisfied smile.

'There we are then,' the companion said. 'Now you must not weary yourself, milady. Perhaps you should leave her now, Miss Wainwright. You can see Her Ladyship is in no condition to talk at the moment.'

'We shall have a longer chat another time,' Charity said.

Lady Merton smiled. 'You will send for the vicar now, Miss Monteith,' she said.

'That I will. And perhaps you could convince His Lordship to leave the room next door, Miss Wainwright. The noise is bothering Her Ladyship.'

'What is John doing in the gold guest room?' Lady Merton asked.

'He has been giving me a little tour of the house, ma'am. I shall ask him to show me the downstairs, as you are trying to rest.'

'It is a fine old house,' Lady Merton said, 'but not a happy one, I fear. The watercolor of the cloisters in the gold room next door was done by my sister, Lady Holcroft, when she visited me in the last century. That little shadow in the fifth archway is the singing nun. Beth, my sister, saw her.'

'How interesting. I shall take a good look at it another time. Now I shall leave you.'

They parted amicably. Charity was convinced Miss Monteith was up to no good. She hastened back to the gold room to tell Lord Merton what had transpired.

He beckoned her to the clothespress. She went on tiptoe, to hide her actions from prying ears in the next room. 'Speak softly. Miss Monteith is listening next door,' she whispered. The clothespress held Lady Merton's winter gowns, moved here for convenience for the coming summer.

'Feel this,' Merton whispered.

Charity felt a gray merino gown. 'It is damp!' she said in a low voice.

'There're traces of a fire in the grate,' Lewis told her. 'We think someone was boiling water there. There is a knothole in the back of the clothespress, with a hole in the wall behind it, and another little hole leading right into Mama's clothespress. With a hose stuck in the kettle spout to direct—'

'Her ghost was steam!' Charity said. 'She had another visitation last night. Let us go

53

belowstairs to discuss this.'

They walked as silently as they could to the staircase and down to the Blue Saloon.

'Lady Merton asked me to try to remove her ghost,' Charity said. 'She admitted to some wrongdoing in her past, but with Miss Monteith listening in, I could not press for details. I hope to have a private talk with her soon.'

'I wish you luck,' Lewis said. 'I have been trying to get her alone to ask for an advance on my allowance for a week. Monteith sticks like a barnacle. She don't let Mama stir an inch without her.'

'I shall arrange it,' Merton said. 'Perhaps this evening. I wonder when those holes were poked in the clothespresses and in the wall between them.'

'You cannot blame old Monteith for that,' Lewis said. 'That peephole has been there forever. I used to spy through it to see where Mama was hiding my birthday present when I was a lad. She usually hid it under the bed.'

'As Miss Monteith was an upstairs maid, no doubt she was aware of it and decided to put it to use,' Merton said. 'I shall have the holes plugged up this very day. And I shall have the attic window nailed shut while I am about it.' He went to the hallway and spoke to Bagot, the butler.

When he returned, he said, 'Mama has asked the vicar to call this afternoon. Bagot will take care of the holes and the window while she is belowstairs for the visit. Monteith usually accompanies her.'

'What, St John coming again?' Lewis scowled. 'He will be moving in bag and baggage next thing we know. I say, John, you don't think *he* could be working with Monteith?'

Lord Merton rolled his eyes ceilingward. 'I think we can assume the vicar is innocent, Lewis. Mama's fit of vapors is more troublesome to him than to anyone else. She quite relies on his support. We have never had any trouble with St John. An excellent chap.'

Lewis said aside to Charity, 'He is our cousin. John gave him the living.'

As there was nothing else to be done at the moment, Lewis offered to take Miss Wainwright on a tour of the grounds. She was sorry she had accepted when she noticed that Merton looked a little disappointed.

Her spirits were restored when Merton called after them, 'You might take Miss Wainwright to the stable to pick out a mount, Lewis.' He turned to Charity. 'I took the liberty of sending a footman off to London for your riding habit early this morning, ma'am. With luck he should be back by this evening.' He had remembered! The speed of his action suggested he was very eager for that ride.

The walk with Lewis was about what she expected. He knew virtually nothing about the architecture and the gardens of the house. When she dallied in the rose garden, he flicked a bloom and said, 'Those are roses, I believe. Yes, that's it. I've been pricked by a thorn. Curst things. I cannot imagine why Mama wants a gardenful of thorns.'

Her questions about the landscaping of the park were met with a similar lack of knowledge or interest. There was said to be a Judas tree planted to mark the execution of Charles I, but Lewis had no notion of which tree it might be.

'Someone called Reptile, or Repton, or some such thing did the place up years ago. I daresay he chopped it down. He made a mess of the place. Put in that little stream you see there and clumped the trees in threes. I shall show you where I fish for trout.' Lewis the poet would have shown her a more interesting tour, but he had decided poetry was dull stuff after all when compared to hunting for ghosts in a dandy satin-lined cape.

About the only area they were both interested in was the stable. Merton did indeed keep an excellent one. There were twenty stalls occupied, counting Mr Wainwright's team. Well-muscled brown and black flanks gleamed in the sunlight. A pair of grooms tended the horses, brushing them and leading one pair out for exercise. Charity tentatively chose a bay mare called Charmer for her mount. When they espied the vicar's gig driving through the park, they decided to return to the house to oversee the patching up of the holes in the clothespresses and the wall between.

CHAPTER FIVE

'About as much fun as watching grass grow' was Lewis's opinion of watching the estate carpenter putty up the holes in the clothespresses and the wall between them. 'Let us see what your papa is up to instead.'

They found Wainwright in the library poring over yellowed and sere documents pertaining to the history of Keefer Hall.

'Have you found any more ghosts, sir?' Lewis asked.

'An interesting account of the ravens,' Wainwright replied. 'I had heard of them before, of course. It is said they have been here since the execution of Charles I.'

'Really? That long!' Lewis exclaimed. 'I had no idea ravens were such long livers.'

'Not the same birds, Lord Winton, but six ravens.'

'Ah, hatched right there on the roof, no doubt.'

Mr Wainwright did not like to have his dramatic soliloquies interrupted by the audience. He lowered his black brows and continued. 'Birds are frequently harbingers of luck, either ill or good. At Longleat it is said the family will die out if the swans that nest on the lakes of Longleat ever leave.'

'Yes, I have heard that old canard—er, legend—forever.' Lewis nodded.

'At Radley Hall, where I was doing my research last year—perhaps you read my extract? No? I have a copy in my room if you would like to have a glance at it. At Radley Hall the swans fly around the house to foretell a death. There are black swans at Radley. There was a theory that unwonted activity of black birds foretold death. The ravens here at Keefer Hall throw that theory askew. What I have found in this account of Sir Nicholas Dechastelaine, your great-uncle—'

'You never want to believe anything Uncle Nick said. Drunk or sober, he never told the truth in his life.'

'Indeed!' Wainwright exclaimed, aghast at the fellow's impertinence. 'It is pretty well documented that the ravens have been circling the house in a frenzy to foretell good luck for nigh on two hundred years—numerous victories at war, births, marriages. They flew when the Royalists took Marlborough in 1642. Your ancestor, Lord Whitby Dechastelaine, led a regiment in that campaign. And again in 1745 when another Dechastelaine took part in the British victory at Louisburg in Canada. Various of Admiral Nelson's victories, too. Word of those triumphs did not reach Keefer Hall for months, but the ravens knew. They

58

flew on the dates of the occurrences. The account goes on for pages, documenting not only issues of national importance, but family births and marriages, as I mentioned. Your mama will know if the ravens flew at the time of her marriage.'

'I shall ask her.' Lewis was more interested in ghosts than in birds and said, 'Have you found any more ghosts?'

'I am just looking for confirmation of my feeling that Knagg and the Ironside ghost are related by blood. It is bound to be here someplace.'

Lewis poked through a few books, then came up with a different idea. 'Perhaps you would like to see the secret panel, Mr Wainwright, and the priest's hole? We call it a priest's hole, but as we never were Papists I daresay it actually had something to do with hiding from Cromwell's men.'

'I took the liberty of investigating the secret panel and the priest's hole earlier, Lord Winton. Lady Merton was kind enough to tell me to make myself at home. Very interesting, but there are no ghosts there.'

'How did you find them?' Lewis demanded. 'Mama did not leave her room until Vicar arrived.'

Wainwright just smiled. 'I knew where they were. Something beckoned to me. I have a sixth sense regarding such matters.'

His daughter suspected he had also taken a

glance at the plans of the house. Three long cylindrical tubes of the sort that often held house plans sat on the table where he was working.

'By Jove!' Lewis exclaimed. 'Would you like to see them, Miss Wainwright?'

'Indeed I would.'

'We shall do it after lunch. It is a bit late to begin now. I daresay you will want to brush out your pretty hair. Not that it needs it. Or your long eyelashes or your satiny cheeks either,' he added foolishly.

Charity was too kind to state the obvious: that she never brushed her eyelashes or cheeks. 'My hands are a little dusty,' she said, and darted upstairs.

The vicar, St John, remained for lunch. Charity feared the meal would be an uneasy one. Vicars often took her papa's interest in ghosts amiss. Fortunately, St John was not adamant on the matter.

'There were instances of ghostly apparitions in the Old Testament,' he mentioned. 'Saul's visit to the witch of Endor comes to mind. Samuel the prophet materialized. And of course during the witch trials of the Middle Ages there were various appearances of spirits.'

Lord Merton was unhappy with this wanton encouragement of his mama's folly. 'I had not expected a man of the cloth to hold such views, St John,' he said.

Lady Merton bridled up like an angry mare. 'Are you saying I am mad, Merton?' she asked. 'I know what I saw.'

'I doubt you will be bothered by these "ghosts" again, Mama,' he said.

'I hope you may be right,' she said doubtfully.

'I am right.' He stared across the table at Miss Monteith. 'I have taken certain steps, and if any more spirits come to harass you, I am ready to take further action. Now can we not discuss something more tangible? How is the St Alban's fund coming along, Vicar?'

'The kind ladies of the parish are holding a sort of spring bazaar. The proceeds of that will, I hope, take care of the necessary repairs to the perishing stonework in the church tower. You know it is my hope to build up an emergency fund. There are times when money is required on the spot, as it were. The horrible fire that consumed the Danson residence comes to mind. Six children—fortunately all survived, but for that poor widow to have to start from scratch, outfitting a house and six children—I wished I could have done more for her.'

He shook his head sadly. Sadness seemed to come naturally to him. He was all skin and bones, like a tuppenny rabbit. A tall, austere gentleman with wispy blond hair, pale blue eyes, a long nose, and a weak chin.

'Your contribution was most welcome,' he added to Merton. 'Very generous, to be sure, but had it occurred while you were in London—well, you see why I am eager to have an emergency fund at my disposal.'

The vicar went to the library with Wainwright after lunch to look over the family documents pertaining to ghosts. Lord Merton suggested that his mama go for a drive, hoping the spring sunshine would raise her spirits.

'Yes, I would like to drive into the village,' she said. 'I have a little business to attend to.'

'Miss Wainwright will accompany you,' Merton said with a meaningful glance at Charity.

She assumed this was an effort to get Lady Merton away from Miss Monteith, to allow her to confess her past transgression. 'I would be happy to accompany you, ma'am,' she said at once.

Lady Merton showed only lukewarm pleasure. 'You are entirely welcome to come with us, my dear, but I fear you would be bored. I really do not feel up to visiting the shops or anything of that sort. I have to see my man of business, Mr. Penley.'

That 'us' suggested Miss Monteith was going along.

'There you are then,' Lewis said. 'We can investigate the secret panels and so on, as we planned, Miss Wainwright.'

'That will be more amusing for you,' Lady Merton said at once, and left.

Merton gave a grimace at Miss Monteith's

retreating back. 'The woman is worse than a burr. I wonder what mysterious "business" Mama has to take care of.'

Lewis said, 'Arranging to give St John money for his charity, I daresay. I know she has been giving him plenty. When I asked her for that advance, she said her pocket was to let. She has not bought a new bonnet or gown for two years. What else could she be doing with her blunt?'

'Very likely she contributed something for the Dansons,' Merton mentioned. 'Yet she would hardly have to visit her man of business for such a trifle as that. . . .'

Lewis gave a quick frown. 'I hope she ain't planning to hand over my fortune to that trust fund St John is always nattering about.'

'She would not do that,' Merton said. 'Yet it is odd she is visiting Penley. I shall have a word with the vicar about this trust fund before he leaves.'

'Then we are off,' Lewis said, offering Charity his arm.

Merton gave his brother a sharp glance. 'You have weighed the wool from the shearing and arranged for its removal to Eastleigh, Lewis?'

'Eh? No, how could I? I have been busy all morning.'

'The wool is your responsibility.'

'But what about Miss Wainwright? Dash it, John, she is our guest.'

'I can look after myself,' Charity said, feeling she was a burden on the family. 'In fact, I should see if Papa needs me. Very likely he has copious notes for me to copy.' She rose to go after her father.

Merton placed a restraining hand on her wrist. 'No, no, you wish to see the secret panels. I will be happy to show them to you.'

'I do not want to be a burden on anyone. I am quite accustomed to looking after myself.'

'I fear I have already offended Mr Wainwright by my lack of faith in ghosts. It would be unconscionable of me to offend both my guests. You must allow me to do the pretty, Miss Wainwright.'

There was some teasing manner in the speech that made her uncomfortable. Merton seemed unaware of it, however. He turned to Lewis and said, 'Well, what are you waiting for? That load of wool ain't going to get to town by itself.'

Lewis decided a trip into Eastleigh would offer some amusement. 'I shall take a peek in Penley's window while I am there and see if Mama is giving St John my fortune.'

'Has Mr Wainwright taught you to hear through walls?' Merton asked.

He did not observe the angry sparkle in Charity's eyes. She had no argument with his lack of belief in ghosts, but when he derided her father in this way, he was going too far.

'Lord Winton said window, milord,' she

snipped. 'It would require lipreading for that, would it not? Unfortunately, reading lips is not one of my father's accomplishments.'

'I am sorry,' he said at once. 'But you must admit, Miss Wainwright, these notions of your father are a load of rubbish. No sane person can actually believe in ghosts.'

'Then you are calling your mama mad as well,' she pointed out.

'No, merely overly prone to suggestion. We know someone has been playing tricks on her. I do not suggest your papa is involved, for he only arrived yesterday and this has been going on for a month, but I fear his presence aggravates the situation. Ah, here is St John!' he said, as the sound of footfalls in the hallway was heard.

Charity had no time to reply, but she felt an angry burning sensation in her breast.

Merton went to the doorway. 'Have you a moment, St John?' he asked.

The vicar entered the saloon with a shy, tentative step. 'About this St Alban's Trust Fund,' Merton said. 'Exactly how is it set up? Who is in charge of the money?'

'The board of directors, milord.'

'And you are the president of the board?'

'Why, yes. That is the arrangement.'

'Who is the treasurer?'

St John blinked in perplexity. 'You are, milord. Do you not recall, when the fund was set up last year, you were kind enough to assume the role of treasurer? Squire Lockhead is the secretary.'

'Ah! Just so.' A trace of pink was noticeable around Merton's jaw. 'It had slipped my mind as we never seem to have any meetings.'

'It is all very informal. You are busy, milord. I handle the day-to-day business. The spring bazaar and so on.'

'Yes, yes. I understand. I just wondered, as you mentioned it at lunch.'

'Was there anything else, milord?'

'No. That is all. Thank you for your time. I shall make a point to attend the bazaar.'

The vicar bowed himself out and Merton scowled at Lewis. 'That was demmed embarrassing. I told you St John was innocent.'

'I never said he wasn't!' Lewis shrugged. 'I only said Mama might be planning to give him my fortune.' He explained to Charity, 'Since there are no girls in the family, Mama has left her money to me in her will. Ten thousand pounds. Merton is already rich as a nabob. As St John is our cousin, and poor as a church mouse, she might feel sorry for him is all I meant.'

'You implied he was weaseling around to get her money for his trust fund,' Merton said.

Before the brothers came to cuffs, Charity tried to smooth the waters. 'The vicar does not look like you two. Nor like Lady Merton either.'

66

'He ain't a real cousin,' Lewis told her. 'That is to say, he was adopted by the St Johns at birth. They are our cousins. They live just a few miles away. Although he could be some kin, I daresay. Cousin Algernon cut a few capers in his day.'

'It is possible, but unlikely,' Merton said. 'The vicar was born somewhere near Keefer Hall. The St Johns were an aging couple, childless. They raised him as a son and a gentleman. He attended university and so on, but unfortunately had no money left to him.'

Charity listened, trying to piece together the relationship. 'As he lived nearby, is it possible he would know what is bothering your mama, Lord Merton? Perhaps that is why she chose him for her confidant.'

'How could he know? He is not much older than myself.'

'Surely he is much older than you!'

'No, he is younger than he looks. It is his shuffling manner that ages his appearance.'

'He will certainly outlive Mama,' Lewis said. 'And if he goes on with these insinuating visits, he will diddle me out of a couple of thousand at least. Well, I am off. What was it I was supposed to do again, John? Oh, yes, the demmed wool. And keep an eye on Mama, too.'

He left. Charity judged by his insouciant whistle that he was not too concerned about losing his fortune to St John.

'Shall we have a look at the secret panels now?' Merton said, and put his hand on Charity's elbow to lead her off.

CHAPTER SIX

'Will we not require lamps?' Charity said.

'There speaks the voice of experience,' Merton replied. 'I see our priest's hole and secret panel will be no thrill for you, Miss Wainwright. I have not been down the stairs for years myself.'

'There are stairs! That will be something new at least. Where do they lead?' She watched as Merton's long, graceful fingers fiddled with the flint and wick. A carved emerald ring gleamed on his left hand as he took up a lamp.

'That would spoil the surprise,' he replied. 'I fear I am giving you undue expectations. It is really a very dull staircase.'

'How spoiled you are. A secret staircase, and you not only ignore it for years, you actually call it dull!'

'You are thinking of Pope, the poet, I wager. About to bethump me with the old cliche that all things look yellow to the jaundiced eye.'

'You put words in my mouth, milord. What I was about to say was that if I had such a thing at home, I would run up and down it ten times a day.'

'When I was a child, I behaved as a child,' he said with a grin. 'Now that I am a man, I have put away childish behavior. There is an insult for you in there if you look hard enough.'

Charity was surprised to discover that Merton was more conversable than she had thought. She decided a little gentle teasing might do him good. 'An enjoyment of harmless pleasures should not die with childhood. We all require diversion from time to time.'

'Running an estate of this size leaves but little time for diversion. In my free moments I can usually find something more amusing than running up and down a staircase.'

'If you would rather be doing something else, I can go alone.'

'Good lord, that was not my meaning! I shall be seeing it with an attractive young lady. In such company the activity is secondary. That is a compliment, ma'am, to make up for my former insult.' He noticed, however, that neither insult nor compliment had much effect on her. 'Quite an occasion in my Spartan existence,' he added.

'Odd that men speak of Spartans as if they were the height of manhood, yet it was the more urbane, pleasure-loving Athenians who overcame Sparta in the end. A Spartan life leaves no room for the imagination.'

Merton lifted the lamp and headed for the morning parlor and the priest's hole. 'I see you are adept at debate,' he replied with a smile.

'An unusual talent in a young lady. I wonder what can account for it.'

She frowned. 'Papa's society has lively debates. I wonder what manner of young lady you have been associating with, if they cannot hold up their end of a discussion.'

'Perhaps they can, but they don't, when they are with an eligible *parti*.'

Charity felt her experience in the field of flirtation was lacking. Her mama had died when she was young; she had never made her debut or had a really close female friend with whom she could discuss the important matter of nabbing a husband. Was she doing something wrong? Was that why her young gentlemen never came up to scratch? She said, 'How *do* they behave?'

'They agree. They simper. They praise. They ask sly questions. You missed an excellent opportunity to discover the extent of my estate just now.'

'I already know it. I looked you up in the *Peerage* before leaving London.'

A choking sound came from Merton's throat. It increased in volume until it was a full-blown laugh. 'I see. Very sensible.'

'Then why are you laughing at me?' she asked sharply.

'There is nothing so amusing as the truth. I was not laughing at you, but at the foolish hypocrisy that exists between the sexes.'

'I know perfectly well you were laughing at
70

me, but let us not spoil this delightful diversion by arguing.'

'I see you will be easy to entertain, Miss Wainwright. You must consider the moldy cellars and dusty attics at your disposal, to enjoy yourself to the top of your bent.'

'Oh, not cellars! There might be rats there.'

'I daresay there are bats in the secret passage.'

Charity felt a frisson down her spine. 'You are trying to frighten me! I do not mind spiders. One can always step on them, but bats! Ugh!'

'Here we are,' he said, setting down his lamp and pulling back an edge of carpet in the corner of the morning parlor. 'The priest's hole. In the old days it had a cabinet over it, to hide the trapdoor. The cabinet moved aside to let the guilty party slip into the hole. The cabinet was then replaced until whoever was looking for him left. An excellent place for a ghost! All it would require is for someone to forget to remove the cabinet and the poor soul would be there until he died.'

He slid his fingers into the hollowed-out groove and lifted the door. There was a little cube not more than five feet all around, with a bench built into the side of it. Unless he was shorter than five feet, the person who was hiding had to sit down.

Charity looked in at a dusty floor with a tin soldier in one corner. 'Lord Winton has been here,' she said. 'This is a very inferior priest's

71

hole, milord. At Radley Hall they had spiders and black beetles, to say nothing of cobwebs.'

Merton frowned at a little pile of what looked like sawdust on the floor. 'If you look very hard, you might find termites,' he said. 'Damme, I must have this sprayed with chlorine to kill the beetles. Shall we move along to the *pièce de résistance*?'

'Yes, please.'

Merton lowered the door, replaced the carpet, then he took up his lamp and they returned to the Blue Saloon. 'Why did we not begin here, as we were in this room?' Charity asked.

'Foolish question. One does not begin with the *pièce de résistance*. It is always kept for the last. We Spartans eat the cake before the icing—but we do get around to the choice bits eventually.' His eyes moved slowly over her face as he spoke, lingering on her lips.

'I wish you would not stare at me like that! It makes me feel as if I were the cake.'

'No, the icing,' he murmured provocatively.

A blush rose up from her collar. 'You are wondering whether propriety demands a setdown. It don't,' he said.

'You are behaving most improperly, Lord Merton,' she said primly.

'No, no. Not *most* improperly. That will come later, after we have enjoyed the cake.'

After this leading speech, he went directly to a far corner, clothed in shadows, and began examining a cupboard built into the wall. He opened the lower doors of the cupboard, knelt down, and removed some dusty bowls and books. 'You have to get on your hands and knees to get in,' he explained. Charity frowned at her gown. 'No doubt things were better organized at Radley Hall,' Merton said. He began poking around the now empty cavity of the cupboard. 'How the devil does this thing work?' he asked, presumably of himself.

'You mean you don't know? Upon my word, you treat your architectural treasures in a very cavalier manner.'

'I come from a long line of Cavaliers,' he replied.

Charity gave him a blighting stare for this poor pun. 'There is a drawer above the bottom doors. Would the drawer be the key to getting into the passage?'

'Yank it out,' he said.

When she pulled out the drawer, Merton hollered. 'Wait until I get my fingers out!'

'You told me to open it!'

She removed the drawer while Merton massaged his crushed fingers. 'That's it!' he exclaimed. 'The passage has opened. It slides open as the drawer is pulled out. I remember now.'

'I do not see how you could have forgotten,' she said, crouching down to examine the open passage. 'I shall ruin my gown. Look at the dust!'

73

'What, no dust at Radley Hall?' He was already crawling through the opening, into a small chamber with stairs leading up. When Charity handed him the lamp, he looked around. 'It is as well you are not frightened of spiders' was all he said.

Charity climbed through the opening. 'Where does this lead?' she asked, looking at the staircase.

'To the attic.'

'That is all? Just to the attic? I thought it would lead to a bedchamber. The old lords frequently had such a contraption to allow them to visit ladies—ladies other than their wives, I mean,' she added.

Merton grinned. 'We Dechastelaines do not go in for that sort of thing.'

She peered at him askance. 'Lewis mentioned a cousin Algernon...'

'Cousin Algernon was the exception that proves the rule. Actually, the family has quite a few exceptions that prove the rule. Like French grammar, in fact. More exceptions than rules.'

'It certainly sounds very French.'

They began climbing up the stairs, Merton leading the way with his lamp held high.

'I cannot believe there is not a secret door into one of the bedchambers,' Charity said, stopping at the first landing to examine the walls. She could find no suspicious woodwork, however. The walls appeared to be solid enough.

74

'This leads only to the attic, and an unfinished part of the attic at that. There are no floors, just the cross members, with the ceiling of the bedroom below, made of lathe and plaster. Not strong enough to take a person's weight, as I discovered in my youth.'

'What is the point of such a secret passage?' she asked.

'I've no idea. Perhaps the passage was never completed, or perhaps it was only used for concealing treasure. I understand the silverplate and some paintings and gold were concealed here during Cromwell's rampage. That makes the passage worthwhile, does it not?'

'In a purely rational way I daresay it does—that would be reason enough for *you*. There is not much food here for the emotions. No frisson scuttles up the spine, no hair stands on end.'

Merton noticed a movement out of the corner of his eye. He said, 'If you really want your hair standing on end, I think I can provide that as well. There is—'

Charity saw where he was looking and glanced up to see three small bats hanging from the rafters. A shriek split the air. 'Bats!' she exclaimed, and threw her hand over her head to protect her hair. Her shout roused one of them from its sleep. It spread its wings slowly. As she shrieked and tried to hide behind Merton, he swept her protectively to his chest and began looking around for a shelf to hold the lamp, so he could put this interlude to full use. Charity clutched at his waist, burrowing her head into his shoulder.

'Quiet!' he cautioned. 'They were asleep. It is your shouting that is waking them. Damme, one of them is coming toward us,' he lied, chewing back a grin.

'Stop him! Oh, but don't kill him! Let us go!'

She looked up and saw the laughter in his eyes. She looked up at the dark corner and discerned the three inert forms. In the close shadows of the little landing, she was suddenly very aware that she was still clutching at Merton's waist. Strangely, she forgot all about the bats. His face was close to hers. His free arm encircled her protectively, while the lamp in his other hand cast flickering shadows around them. She felt his breath fan her cheek. They stood for a moment, each very conscious of the other's proximity. When Merton's arm began to tighten around her, Charity became aware of the impropriety of her situation and dropped her arms. 'They seem to have settled down,' she said.

'Pity. You rob me of the heroic role of bat slayer. Shall we have a nice argument about the unnecessary killing of bats, or would you rather go on up to the attic?'

Charity cleared her throat uneasily. 'I really should see if Papa needs me.'

'I shall never understand you, Miss

Wainwright,' Merton said, shaking his head. 'How can you take ghosts in your stride and be frightened of a little bat?'

'You are talking about two completely different things. You ignore the very possibility of ghosts, when hundreds of people say they have seen them. You have no imagination. Perhaps I have too much. I could almost imagine that bat was clawing into my hair.'

'That is superstition. Bats do not nest in ladies' hair.'

'Of course they do. Everyone knows that.'

'I do not know it. I know! I am not everyone,' he added hastily.

'I was going to say they are nasty, dirty things, whether they nest in one's hair or not,' she said, and ran quickly down the staircase, where she scrambled out of the cupboard as fast as her legs could carry her.

While Merton returned the dusty bowls and books, Charity complained of her gown. 'I knew I would get my gown dusty.'

'The servants will clean it for you.'

She went up to her room at once. While she changed her gown, she discovered she had to reassess Lord Merton. He was not entirely given over to work by any means. In fact, he was nothing short of a delightful flirt. But what were his intentions? This visit was turning out to be more interesting than she had anticipated. As no one was about when she came down, she went in search of her papa and was told by Bagot that he had gone to investigate the cloisters. She eventually found him at the rear of the house, strolling through a covered archway that surrounded a paved quadrangle. A series of ten graceful stone arches in the Norman style formed the outer wall.

'Ah, there you are,' he said, smiling, when he saw her. 'A marvelous place. The singing nun is at home here. She is the same lady who was stabbed in Lord Merton's room. I have been trying to get a grasp of why it happened. I am beginning to wonder if there is a link between her and Knagg and the Cromwellian ghost. A lovers' triangle, as it were. That would heighten the animosity between Knagg and the other ghost. His name is Charles, by the by, but he calls himself Walter. He did not want to have the same name as the king, whom he despised.'

'Did you find any confirmation of this in the library?' she asked. It darted into her head that he may have found the story there and put it forth as his own, to be 'confirmed' at a later date. Such little ruses were not beneath him.

'No, but I shall keep on digging. I would like to visit Lord Merton's bedchamber again. Lady Merton told me to make myself at home.'

'I would ask Merton first, Papa,' Charity said.

'I saw him ride off a while ago. I hailed him,

but he did not hear me. I shall just run up and have a quick look. There can be no harm in it. I was in there last night.'

'I wish you would wait until he returns.'

'What is the harm in it? I shan't touch anything. Come along, Charity. I want you to take notes for me. I sometimes forget the exact words of the speaker. I want an accurate record.'

Charity tried again to dissuade him, but when he became sharp with her, she went along. Knowing that Merton had ridden out, it seemed superfluous to knock at the door. Mr Wainwright just opened it and barged in, with Charity behind him. They both found themselves staring at a very surprised Lord Merton, caught in the act of undressing. His shirt was off, revealing a handsome set of shoulders and a patch of dark hair on his broad chest. His valet was handing him a clean shirt.

'What is the meaning of this?' Merton exclaimed angrily.

'I was sure you had left, milord,' Wainwright said. 'I saw you—well, it must have been Lord Winton, I daresay.'

Charity beat a hasty retreat. From a few yards down the hall she heard Merton's angry tirade. 'And you came snooping about my room the moment I was gone! This is intolerable!'

'I was just looking for the singing nun,' Mr Wainwright said apologetically, backing from the doorway. 'Another time.'

'This room is out of bounds for your witch hunting, sir, at any time!'

'*Ghost* hunting, milord!' Wainwright said.

'Get out!'

Wainwright closed the door and joined his daughter.

'I told you you should ask him,' Charity said. Shame turned her cheeks as red as boiled beets. She feared this would be the end of Lord Merton's interest in her. He thought she and her papa were a pair of nosy, snooping commoners—if not worse. First Papa had failed to find Lady Merton's ghost; now he had given Lord Merton a disgust of them. They must certainly leave at once, before they were requested to go. She gave a hint of her feelings.

'No, he does not want us to leave,' Wainwright said. 'Lord Merton is hot at hand; he was surprised but not really angry.'

'He told you to get out!'

'Aye, but I sensed he regretted it almost before the words were out. I shall explain, but I shall not apologize. That is for Merton to do. Now, the Armaments Room requires more work.'

Bagot, his long legs moving like pistons, came running to meet them as they descended the stairs. 'Mr Wainwright! Mr Wainwright, come! The Armaments Room is a shambles. I heard a great crashing sound and went to investigate. The table holding the yellow jerkin and the helmet has been overturned by Knagg. There was no one in the room when it happened.'

'Come!' Wainwright shouted gleefully, and darted off to the Armaments Room, with Charity in hot pursuit.

CHAPTER SEVEN

The scene in the Armaments Room was as Bagot had described it. The small table holding the antique pistols, the round helmet, and the jerkin had been overturned, its contents scattered about the floor.

'Can you not feel it?' Wainwright exclaimed. 'The anger of those two blood relatives! It is overwhelming. I must ask you to leave, Charity. You might be harmed. Bagot, you will speak to the servants and determine that no one was in this room when the table was toppled. Leave me now. It is time for communication with the spirits.' He closed his eyes and went into what looked like a trance.

Bagot ran off to do as he was bid, while Charity found herself at loose ends. She did not even want to be in the house when Merton came down. To escape, she went out to the cloisters to think. Merton would not be so uncivil as to ask them to leave before morning. She hoped her riding habit had arrived by then, so she could take it home with her; otherwise she would be without it for a few days in London and she wanted to ride. In London riding was restricted to the slow pace of Rotten Row. She had been looking forward to a good run in the country with Merton. How he must despise her now!

She gazed out at the countryside she would not be riding through. Terraced gardens led down from the cloisters, with the land of Keefer Hall spreading away in the distance. There were patches of light and dark green fields, where the various crops were growing under the spring sun. In the farther distance she spied what must be sheep in a meadow, although they did not look like sheep from this distance, perhaps because they had just been sheared. They looked like little pink rocks, except that some of them were moving. A man on a bay mount was riding along the western edge of the field. As he drew closer, she recognized Lord Winton.

Despite the physical resemblance, he was an altogether different sort of person from his elder brother. One would never have to tell him to enjoy himself. He took life very lightly—too lightly, really. Merton was always jawing at him. It was strange that the two brothers were so different. More like father and son than brothers. The *Peerage* had indicated that their father had died some twelve years before, when the present Lord Merton was eighteen, younger than Lewis was now. Merton had had to assume the mantle of responsibility at a youthful age. Perhaps that accounted for his arrogant manner.

In a short while Lewis came out of the stable on foot and discovered Charity. He was not tardy in joining her.

'What a wretched host my brother is, leaving you moping alone,' he said, shaking his head. 'I thought he was going to show you the secret passage.'

'He did. I am not moping.'

'You look as sour as a Methodist. What has happened?'

'Your brother and my papa have come to cuffs,' she said, and explained about the trip to Merton's room.

'Well, if that ain't just like John, to go making a mountain out of a molehill. I shall have a word with him.'

'No, I wish you will not. It is his not believing in ghosts, I think, that makes him impatient with this visit.'

'Dash it, the house is alive with ghosts. How can he not believe? I have a good mind to prove it to him.'

'Perhaps Knagg's latest visit in the Armaments Room will convince him,' she said, but she did not believe it.

Lewis was on his feet. 'Eh? Knagg paid us another visit?'

'Yes, he was very violent this time. He threw

the table over.'

'By gad! Let us go and have a look!' He grabbed her hand, urging her to a faster pace as they returned to the house.

Wainwright had finished his communication with the ghosts. Lord Merton had joined him in the Armaments Room. Bagot was there as well. Charity glanced fearfully at Merton, expecting scowls and sneers. In her considerable astonishment he was smiling and speaking civilly to her papa.

'If Bagot says none of the servants was here, then it must have been Knagg cutting up a lark,' he said in a hearty voice. He spotted Charity and Lewis as they entered. She discerned a trace of embarrassment in his manner when he looked at her. It was there, in his uncertain smile and proud head, which was held a fraction lower than usual.

'Ah, Lewis, you will want to have a look at this. Mr Wainwright has suggested we leave the table and items on the floor as they are for the nonce, to see if the ghosts separate the items. You will see the yellow jerkin is resting on a Cavalier's pistol. Mr Wainwright thinks Knagg will move it. He plans to lock the room to ensure that no one—no living person, I mean—interferes. That would certainly convince *me* that we have ghosts.' He did not dare to look at Charity as he uttered this plumper, but he was acutely aware that she was staring at him.

'The windows must be secured as well,' Wainwright explained. Merton looked doubtful at this. He was repentant, but he did not intend to have his window frames fitted out with locks to keep out nonexistent ghosts. 'Putty,' Wainwright explained. 'It can be removed without leaving a trace.'

Merton said, 'Just so. Bagot, you will see to it.'

'Certainly, your lordship.' Bagot left reluctantly.

'Well, this is certainly an amazing example of ghostly work, is it not, Mr Wainwright?' Merton continued. 'You will want to write this up for the Ghost Society, I wager.'

'That is the Society for the Study of Discarnate Beings,' Wainwright corrected him. 'There are other spirits besides ghosts. I am in contact with a Herr Schmidt from Berlin who is doing fascinating work on what he calls *polter geists*. The phrase means noise ghosts. They are unusual in that they never materialize but only make their presence known by means of noises. He will certainly be interested in today's occurrence, but I think we have your ordinary run-of-the-mill ghosts here at Keefer Hall, not *polter geists*. The reason I say so is that I actually caught a glimpse of Charles this afternoon. Walter I should call him, the Cromwellian ghost. A handsome enough fellow, but with a polt foot.' His audience stared at him in confusion. 'A clubfoot, we call it nowadays, like poor Byron. Walter calls it a polt foot.'

Merton's patience gave out. 'I suggest we all have a glass of sherry to celebrate this occurrence,' he said, and led the others to the Blue Saloon. Wainwright remained behind to commune with the spirits.

As Bagot was occupied with attending to the putty, Merton poured the sherry himself and handed it around.

When they were seated, he cleared his throat and said to Charity, 'I have apologized to Mr Wainwright for my farouche behavior earlier this afternoon, ma'am, and I now wish to apologize to you. I was caught off guard. Being half-dressed, I did not expect company.'

'Good God!' Lewis laughed. 'Did they catch you with your trousers down, John? Miss Wainwright did not tell me *that*! No wonder you was sore as a gumboil.'

Merton's jaw worked silently. He was displeased that Miss Wainwright had confided her troubles to Lewis. 'My trousers were in place. I was changing my shirt, which had become soiled in the secret passage.'

'Being without a shirt ain't any excuse for insulting the Wainwrights,' Lewis said severely. 'Upon my word, you ought to be shown a lesson.'

'I am speaking—apologizing—to Miss Wainwright,' Merton said, flicking an admonishing glance at his brother.

Charity said in a flustered way, 'That is quite all right, milord. I understand. Indeed I feel I ought to apologize myself. I told Papa he should wait and ask your permission.'

Merton agreed with her, but he was so eager to have the matter settled that he said, 'I was certainly more at fault. An Athenian would not have behaved so uncivilly.'

Lewis said, 'Eh? What the deuce do Athenians have to do with it?'

Merton said, 'Nothing. Did you take care of the wool?'

'Of course I did. And I dropped in on Penley, too. Let on I was thinking of buying some Consols. How he could believe that when he knows I haven't a sou to my name ... However, he was pretty worried, John. He asked if you'd drop in on him. He would not tell *me*, of course, but I wager Mama is up to something scatterbrained, like giving my blunt to St John's charity fund.'

'I shall certainly call on him soon.'

'"As soon as possible" is what he actually said. I believe he mentioned something about urgent and a most serious matter. I meant to tell you the instant I got home, but between hearing about you insulting the Wainwrights and Knagg cutting up a fracas, it slipped my mind.'

Merton looked alarmed at this. He set down his glass, drew out his pocket watch, and said, 'I have time to see him before dinner.' Then he turned to Lewis. 'I think this urgent, most serious matter might have taken precedence over a fallen table, Lewis. Has Mama come home?'

'No, I followed her and Monteith. They turned in at the vicarage. No doubt she is going to tell St John he can have my money.'

Without further ado Merton called for his mount and rode into Eastleigh. Charity expected that Lewis would suggest some outing for them, but he seemed distracted.

'It is really the outside of enough,' he muttered into his collar.

'Lord Merton will discover if your fortune is at risk,' she said to console him.

'I ain't talking about that. It is his behavior to you and your papa. Really, the man is a boor. But of course he will look after my money for me. Say that for him. He always does the right thing when money or land is involved,' he said snidely. 'He still don't believe in Knagg, you know. That act in the Armaments Room was a charade to try to smooth your ruffled feathers. Poor John hasn't an iota of imagination.'

'I know.' Charity thought it was rather sweet of Merton to try to pacify her and Papa.

'Did you happen to catch a glimpse of our singing nun when you was down at the cloisters, Miss Wainwright?'

'No, I never see ghosts.'

'What is she supposed to look like? Do you

88

know?'

'The account I glanced at describes her as a young, slender woman with blond hair. She wears a light-colored gown, with a dark stain on the front.'

'I believe I shall take a run out and see if she is there.'

To Charity's relief, he did not invite her to join him. She went for a walk through the park instead, to try to collect her muddled thoughts. She counted four ravens on the roof of the house. A few more were flying about, but not in the frenzied way that foretold good luck. Was it all nonsense? Whatever about the ravens and hauntings at Keefer Hall, it seemed there was a mystery quite unconnected with ghosts. Someone was preying on Lady Merton, and Charity wished to get the lady alone to discover in what manner she was vulnerable. Money had been used to pay for old sins ever since the Middle Ages when wandering friars had sold indulgences. It seemed Lady Merton was attempting to buy redemption. And if she was willing to pay as much as ten thousand pounds for it, it must have been a grievous sin.

Where ladies were concerned, a serious sin was usually sexual in nature. They did not seem to go in much for the gentlemanly offenses of murder or thievery. Had Lady Merton strayed from the path of marital fidelity? The next thing that darted into Charity's head was that either Merton or Winton was an adulterine offspring, with some other father than Lord Merton. If Miss Monteith knew that, she certainly had a very large stick to hold over Lady Merton's head. So large, in fact, that the addition of ghosts to frighten her hardly seemed necessary. Unless Miss Monteith did not have any proof and was preying on her mistress's conscience. That could be it.

She would mention it to Merton—and no doubt receive another blast from his hot temper at the suggestion that he was illegitimate. A soft smile moved her lips. And she would receive another apology, too. How he had hated apologizing. She continued her walk around to the cloisters, expecting to see Lewis, but he had left.

With nothing better to do, she went to the Long Gallery to study the paintings, to see if either Merton or Lewis looked strikingly different from his ancestors. The gentlemen through the ages were all so similar that it seemed impossible either of the brothers could be a by-blow. The crow-black hair and dark eyes, the prominent nose and stubborn chin continued in an unbroken line through the generations. From the fifteenth-century slashed doublets with the lining showing through, to the swaggering short coat and bucket-topped boots of the Cavaliers, to the more restrained black jacket of the present Lady Merton's husband, the men wearing the costumes were similar. The faces and colorings of the wives changed, but the Merton gentlemen were fixed in appearance.

The only other possibility was that Lady Merton had been carrying on with her husband's brother or perhaps a cousin. There was the family rake, Algernon. She doubted that Lady Merton would confess such a thing to a stranger, but she would make the opportunity for a talk at least—if she could ever pry the lady away from Miss Monteith.

CHAPTER EIGHT

Lord Merton did not change the subject immediately when Mr Wainwright mounted his favorite hobbyhorse at dinner that evening. To compensate for his poor behavior earlier, he allowed his guest to ramble on for some time about his experiences at Radley Hall, a place Merton was coming to dislike thoroughly, sight unseen.

Lady Merton had only one concern and only one subject of conversation. 'But you have had no luck with my ghost, Mr Wainwright?'

'I shall have another go at it, madam. My great success with Knagg and Walter gives me hope. It is possible I missed out on something. The nun from Lord Merton's room may have taken to roaming free above stairs. She was not in your chamber when I looked, but that is not

91

to say she is not there from time to time.'

'My ghost is not the singing nun. I wish you will make another attempt to identify her before you leave.'

Strangely, it was Merton who objected to this curt speech, which hinted at an early departure of the Wainwrights. His eyes flew down the board to Charity, whose cheeks were flushed with embarrassment as she gazed at her soup.

'Mr Wainwright will not be leaving soon, I trust. He has a great deal to look into before darting off. We want to get that troublesome business in the Armaments Room settled.'

Lewis smirked. 'Don't forget the ghost in your own room while you are at it, John. I should not be surprised if you see her, as you have suddenly taken up a belief in ghosts.'

'The existence of ghosts has never been disproven, so far as I have heard,' Merton replied blandly.

'No, nor fairies or the bogeyman either, but you do not believe in them.' This came dangerously close to implying that he was not a believer himself. He rushed on to correct this notion. 'Not that I mean to put ghosts in a class with fairies.'

Wainwright did not take offense. On the contrary he said, 'A young fellow called Christopher Hawken is doing some interesting work with leprechauns in Ireland. We at the Society feel they are a branch of the fairy kingdom.'

Miss Monteith took no part in the conversation at table, and Lady Merton took virtually none. The latter was plainly distracted by something. She wore a harried look, as if wrapped up in her own thoughts.

Charity hoped for some privacy with her after dinner, but Miss Monteith accompanied them to the saloon and sat with them until the gentlemen joined them after taking port. Such conversation as occurred was of the most inconsequential. Lady Merton bestirred herself to suggest that Miss Wainwright must be sure to take a drive into Eastleigh. She must also feel free to ride if she wished. Merton or Lewis would see about a mount. As soon as the gentlemen entered the room, Lady Merton rose and said she had a slight megrim and would retire. Miss Monteith rose with her, as if they were attached at the waist.

As Charity was robbed of an opportunity for conversation with Lady Merton, she hoped for some company from Lord Merton. Her father, not much attuned to the problems of living people, asked her to accompany him to the library to write up the few notes he would dictate to her.

'We will be able to hear any disturbance in the Armaments Room room there,' he explained to the others. 'I had the yellow jerkin and the helmet put on another table. We shall see if that satisfied Knagg, or if he insists on

93

removing them from the room altogether. It may come down to that in the end.'

Merton gave a grimacing smile and said nothing about not removing historical artifacts to accommodate a pair of ghosts. Like his mama, he wore a distracted air. Charity was eager to hear what he had learned from Penley. After an hour's undisturbed dictation (the ghosts did not misbehave), she was released from note taking and darted straight back to the Blue Saloon. Lord Merton sat alone before the grate. As he had neither book nor journal, she assumed he was deep in thought.

'Ah, you are free.' He smiled and rose to welcome her.

'Where is Lord Winton?' she asked.

When Merton looked offended, she was sorry she had said it. 'He is about somewhere. Did you particularly wish to see him? I could ask Bagot...'

'Oh, no. I merely wondered.' Merton showed her a seat. 'I hoped to have a private word with Lady Merton, but Miss Monteith stuck like a burr,' she said, shaking her head.

'I spoke to Penley. It is as Lewis fears. Mama is thinking of changing her will, making the St Alban's fund the recipient of half her fortune. I hardly know whether it is my place to try to dissuade her, as it is only half. It is her money after all. Lewis comes into a substantial estate on his twenty-first birthday. He does not need the money. In fact, it is four pence to a groat he will squander it on some foolishness. Perhaps St John would make better use of it.'

'Did you speak to your mama about it?'

'Yes, briefly. She was quite sharp with me. Told me she was just looking into it. Nothing was decided, and if she wished to do it, I could not stop her. No more I can.'

Charity decided this was the moment to broach the notion that had occurred to her that afternoon. She said uncertainly, 'I hope you will not take a pet, Lord Merton, but—'

'Is it not time we dispense with the "Lord," Miss Wainwright?'

'As you wish. No doubt you are familiar with the idea of indulgences.'

He blinked. 'Indulgences? Are you a Papist, ma'am?'

'No, I am speaking of the old days, when people bought indulgences for the forgiveness of their sins.'

'Yes, I see your thinking. Mama has something bearing on her conscience and hopes to buy off hell's fire by giving her money to the church.'

'Exactly! And what could this sin be?'

'I'll be demmed if I know. Let us dispense with this Socratic method of questions and answers. If you have an idea, pray tell me.'

'Socratic method? I thought it was Papa's method! That is how he leads one on to agree with him at the Society. Well, as I was saying, with ladies, the transgression usually has to do

95

with gentlemen, I think. I was just wondering, you know, purely as a speculation, if your mama might have betrayed her husband.'

Merton's displeasure with the suggestion was obvious, but he answered civilly enough. 'Papa certainly had a wandering eye. I never heard any rumor of Mama carrying on with the gents. I do not think it at all likely.'

'She would not feel guilty at her husband's indiscretions, though. That could not account for her guilty feelings.'

'True. Yet five thousand pounds seems a high price to pay for one little slip from the path of rectitude.'

'That would depend on the seriousness of the slip,' she said slyly. 'If there were consequences, serious consequences—a child, I mean—then—'

'Good lord!' Merton sat up, staring at her. 'You think she has a by-blow sequestered somewhere, that she is using this trust fund as a blind to get money to the child!' He rubbed his chin. 'That is not only patently ridiculous but impossible. She never took any suspiciously long trips. She could hardly hide such a thing from Papa, and I promise you he would not have stood still for anything of the sort.'

'You cannot know what happened. You were only a babe at the time—or perhaps not even born. Actually, what I meant was that some gentleman other than Lord Merton was the father of ... of either Winton or yourself, without your papa being aware of it.'

He stared, too dumbfounded to argue for a moment. When he had recovered his wits, he said, 'You're mad!'

'Now do not fly into a pelter, Lord Merton. I only said it is possible.'

'If you had ever seen Papa, you would know this is not possible.'

'You refer to your physical resemblance to him. I have seen him—in a portrait, I mean. Certainly the family likeness is striking, but I daresay he had a brother, or at least cousin Algernon, which could account for the family similarity. Your mama mentioned she had been married for thirty-five years and you are only thirty. That is a long time for her husband to wait for a pledge of her love. She may have been desperate to have a son—to inherit the title and so on.'

'So desperate that she decided to put another man on the job, so to speak? If there is anything at all in this *outrageous* suggestion, you have got the shoe on the wrong foot, Miss Wainwright,' he said stiffly. 'Mama is quite a stickler for the proprieties. If there was any trickery, Papa was the wrongdoer. It is possible *he* has an illegitimate child hidden away somewhere.'

Charity thought about this for a moment. 'Perhaps he asked Lady Merton to see to the child's welfare and she failed to do so. The child died in poverty. Now she feels guilty and is giving the money to St John to give to other unfortunate people.'

'You are forgetting her "ghost" is not Papa, chiding her for her laxity. It is a female.'

She pondered this for a moment. 'It could be the mother of the child. Do you have an elderly relative you might ask about those old days?'

'None living nearby. Nor am I particularly happy to begin spreading such speculations about the countryside. An old family servant would be more discreet.' After a frowning pause, he added, 'Bagot has been with us forever and is a model of discretion. I shall be discreet as well. Let me handle this, ma'am.'

He called Bagot into the saloon. He was a tall, gaunt, elderly man with gray hair that was receding from a high forehead. Bagot was astonished to be invited to take a seat. His rheumy eyes wore a troubled look as he replied, 'I shall remain standing, if it pleases your lordship.'

'Do sit down, Bagot. My neck is stiff from looking up at you.'

Bagot sat on the edge of a chair, his back poker-stiff, looking more uncomfortable than if he had remained standing.

'You will think this a strange question,' Merton began, 'but I want to inquire about the old days at Keefer Hall, when Mama and Papa were first married. You were some sort of junior footman in those days, I believe.'

'Just so, milord. I was born on the estate. I

became backhouse boy at ten years of age.'

'Then you would be aware of any family scandal hovering about the house. Kitchen gossip, that sort of thing.'

'There was no gossip...' He paused, not wishing to give offense. 'That is to say, no more than elsewhere.'

'Papa and Mama never argued? I recall they both had sharp tempers. Come now, Bagot, I could hear them shouting at each other from the nursery.'

'Why, it was all over long before you were born!' Bagot exclaimed.

Charity's heart gave a leap of interest.

Merton said, 'Were those arguments about Papa's flirts?'

'Or Lady Merton's flirts,' Charity added, as she still held to her own opinion on the matter. Merton gave her a quelling look.

Bagot's tongue flicked out to moisten his dry lips. 'Her ladyship did scold a little in the early days. It had to do with Meg, one of the dairymaids, who lived here at Keefer Hall. His lordship had a fondness for her. She was a bonnie lass, blond curls, blue eyes. A forward chit. When her ladyship went home to visit her mama, his lordship elevated Meg to upstairs maid. Your mama did not half like that, when she got home. It was soon apparent that someone...' He glanced uncertainly at Charity.

'Out with it, Bagot,' Merton urged

impatiently.

'Meg became *enceinte*,' he said. 'She was not married. When her condition became noticeable, her ladyship demanded that his lordship turn the girl off. There were arguments about it for some time. In fact, her ladyship did not speak to his lordship for several months. As the *accouchement* drew nigh, her ladyship threatened to leave Keefer Hall if the girl remained. Your papa had no recourse but to be rid of her. He felt sorry for Meg and only sent her to the dower house, which was empty in those days. He did it on the sly, without her ladyship's knowledge, of course. The midwife was called to tend the birth. Meg died in childbirth.'

'What happened to the child?' Merton asked.

'He died as well. They are both buried at the back of the family graveyard.'

'The kitchen gossip was that Papa was the father of Meg's child?' Merton said, hardly making it a question.

'Some said so, your lordship, but Meg had more than one beau dangling after her.'

'Not more than one noble beau, I should think,' Merton said. 'Why would she bother with grooms and footmen if she had caught Papa's eye?'

'It is possible she was already with child when she caught his lordship's eye,' Bagot pointed out. 'Young Meg was not one to miss out on a chance to better herself. She was bold as brass. She developed an overweening manner of ordering the kitchen maids about during her short reign as his lordship's favorite.'

Merton shook his head sadly. 'I hope she enjoyed her brief reign as she paid for it with her life. Thank you, Bagot. That will be all.'

Bagot seemed relieved to be able to stand again and return to his normal duties. 'Shall I pour a glass of wine, milord?'

'Thank you, if you will be so kind.'

Bagot poured the wine while Charity waited on nettles for him to leave so that she might discuss this new revelation with Merton.

Just as Bagot turned to leave, Merton said, 'What was the family name of this Meg, the dairymaid, Bagot? I shall put a bouquet on her grave.'

Bagot gave a startled look. 'Monteith. She was Miss Monteith's sister. And if you want my opinion, the pair of them should have been turned off.' With this speech he bowed and left.

'So that is it!' Charity said in a squeaking voice. 'Miss Monteith is exacting revenge for her sister's death.'

'I shall have a word with Mama. Now that I know the whole story, I may be able to dissuade her from flagellating herself with guilt. I shall tell her Meg Monteith was in the dower house all along, with proper medical care. She is not responsible for the girl's death.

She will be furious with Papa, but anger is better than guilt.'

Lewis joined Charity while she was awaiting Merton's return. Charity sensed an air of excitement about him, but when she inquired what he had been up to, he just yawned into his hand.

'Just dipping into a little poetry. What is new here?'

She outlined the latest discovery. 'By the living jingo, I knew that old malkin of a Monteith was up to no good. I hope John sends her packing. Would you care for a hand of cards while we wait for John to return?'

Merton did not return for thirty minutes, and when he came back, he was scowling.

'Mama refuses to be rid of Miss Monteith,' he said. 'When I threatened to turn her off myself, Mama said she would remove to the dower house, with Monteith to bear her company.'

'But did she deny Bagot's story?' Charity asked eagerly.

'On the contrary, she expanded on it. She was jealous as a green cow of Meg, as she had failed to produce an heir herself. It seems Meg was also uncommonly pretty and bold. Mama says the chit taunted her. Not verbally, but she was bold as brass. Delayed in doing what she was told and so on. To compound the business, it was on the evening of the day Mama got Meg turfed out that the child was born—and we

102

know the consequences.

'It seems Bagot is mistaken about the dower house. Mama says the house was occupied at the time. Papa's cousin Algernon—yes, *that* Algernon—and his wife had been given the use of it for a few months. There was some secrecy in it, which is why the servants did not know. It involved his hiding out after a duel. You may imagine the cause of it. It seems he killed his man and had to rusticate to escape the law. Perhaps his wife was *enceinte* and gave birth while there. In any case, Mama is quite certain Meg was not sent there but turned out with nowhere to go. She has the notion Meg was delivered of her child in an open field without a midwife, which accounts for the mother and child dying. You may be sure Miss Monteith is keeping her guilt at the boil.'

'It don't sound like Mama to be so harsh,' Lewis said.

'She would be if Meg was taunting her,' Charity said. 'No lady would stand for that in her own house.'

'It would not surprise me much if Meg is back, wreaking her own revenge,' Lewis said.

Merton gave him a scalding stare. 'It is news to me if ghosts can boil kettles and poke holes in walls.'

'Why, John, you amaze me!' Lewis said, staring innocently. 'At dinnertime you was all for believing in ghosts. You had best make up your mind. Ah, here is Mr Wainwright now. I

103

daresay you will be a believer again.'

Once Wainwright joined them, the conversation turned to Knagg and other ghostly subjects, until tea was served, and then it was time to retire.

CHAPTER NINE

Two hauntings occurred at Keefer Hall that night. One was not discovered until the next morning; the other caused such a fracas that it kept the occupants of the west wing awake for hours.

Lord Merton, worried about his mama's intransigence in keeping Miss Monteith for her companion, had a deal of trouble getting to sleep at all. He felt it unhealthy for his mama to have this reminder of past wrongdoing constantly before her eyes. He disliked to see five thousand pounds of Lewis's inheritance being whistled down the wind as well, yet his mama (usually so docile) had made it crystal clear that she would brook no interference with her plans.

He had no hope now that Wainwright might rid them of this new 'ghost.' A fellow with a monomania was no new thing to Merton. He had a cousin who wanted to be an Italian; wanted to live in Italy, but as the war made that precarious, he had changed his name from

Joseph Dechastelaine to Giuseppi Mertoni, built himself an Italian villa on the banks of the Thames, staffed it with Italian servants, ate Italian food, built himself a gondola, and read only Italian. He had not exchanged a word with his non-Italian-speaking family for ten years. And good riddance to him!

Foolish as this was, it was at least based in reality. Wainwright's monomania was based on air. Yet it was odd that the yellow jerkin and the round helmet had been thrown to the ground. *Were* there such things as ghosts, or those noise ghosts Wainwright had spoken of? Apparently many otherwise sane folks thought so. The Montagus, for instance. As he tossed and turned, he decided to leave such worries for morning and lull himself to sleep with thoughts of Miss Wainwright.

Her beauty was not of the aggressive sort that leaped out and vanquished a man at first glance. But as he spent more time in her company, he found her softer charms to be insidious. She was not one to flirt or tease or flatter an eligible *parti*. In fact, she had risked his wrath to venture that suggestion that either he or Lewis was an adulterine son. She had quite insisted on it. Really, that was doing it a bit brown! She was not at all the sort of lady a gentleman in his position should consider marrying. She had no particular accomplishments; she boasted no noble connections, and as her papa was a younger son, her dowry would be insignificant.

Yet she was a lively lady. When she smiled, her eyes sparkled. And when she walked, she moved with the grace of a cat. He quite looked forward to riding with her tomorrow. Her riding habit had arrived and been delivered to her room. He would take her through the spinney to the brook, to show her where he used to catch tadpoles. The bluebells should be out by now. It was a pretty spot for ... His eyelids fluttered shut on this happy thought.

It was an hour later that he was aroused from a deep sleep by a crooning chant. His first thought when he opened his eyes was that it was odd the moon was shining in his room. His valet always closed the curtains. And what was that sound ... He sat up and stared all around. There, caught in a shaft of moonlight by his door, stood a woman dressed in some light color. She wore a shawl over her head. As he stared, rubbing his eyes, he thought it was Miss Wainwright. What could account for her coming to his room? Surely she was not that sort of girl!

'Miss Wainwright! Is something wrong?' he asked.

The woman moved a step closer. On the bodice of her gown he noticed a dark smear. A graceful hand moved, pressing the stain. A low moan issued from her throat. Then the hand moved again, pointing to the cold grate.

'There! There he smote me the killing blow.

There I lay, my life blood oozing from me. Ah, pity, pity me, thou unbeliever.'

Her gown, some wispy arrangement of draperies, moved and then she was gone. For a moment Merton sat, stunned into immobility. Good God! It was the singing nun! He had finally seen her. A cold perspiration beaded his brow. Then a second thought urged him into action.

Ghost bedamned! It was some prank of Wainwright's, and if that 'ghost' was not his daughter, he would be much surprised. This was their petty revenge for his belittling their activities. By God, he would not be made a fool of in his own house. He leaped from his bed and ran after her. He was just in time to see the tail of a skirt disappear around the corner of the staircase. He went racing through the dark corridor after the apparition, his bare feet pounding on the carpet.

That alone might not have been sufficient to awaken the occupants of the west wing, but when he reached the stairs, he saw the woman in the entrance hall below, fleeing toward the front door. He ran precipitately down the stairs, taking the steps two at a time. He lost his footing halfway down and fell the remainder of the way, bumping and thumping loudly enough to awaken the dead. When he reached the landing, he fell in a heap, cursing his head off. From the open front door he felt a cold blast of air. She had gotten out, but by God she would not get back in.

He pulled himself up and hobbled painfully, hopping on one foot, to lock the door. He grabbed a blackthorn walking stick from the tall Chinese pot that held a collection of such items and limped back into the hallway just as Bagot appeared, bearing a lamp and wearing a blue satin dressing gown of unlikely pavonine splendor. Merton recognized it vaguely as an old one of his papa's.

'Milord!' Bagot exclaimed, hastening forward, his nightcap tilted rakishly over his left eye.

At the same moment Lewis came darting downstairs, arrayed in a dressing gown of an even more dashing sort. It was a deep wine color, the sash heavily fringed in black. He looked suspiciously wide awake. Lewis was obviously in league with Miss Wainwright in this ill-conceived jape. Merton, turning the air blue with his profanities, limped toward his younger brother.

Abovestairs, Charity had heard the racket and thought her papa must be executing some latenight experiment. She rose, lit her lamp, slipped on a modest dressing gown of blue merino, and tiptoed into the hallway. Her papa's door was closed. When she received no answer to her tap, she opened the door. Mr Wainwright was sleeping peacefully. Should she awaken him? If Knagg was acting up, he would like to know about it. She jiggled his shoulder.

'Papa, wake up. There is some commotion downstairs.'

Mr Wainwright sat up. 'What, what? The spirits are acting up. Excellent! I shall be down presently.'

Charity returned to the hallway. From the top of the staircase she caught a wan ray of light from below and heard raised voices. She was not slow to recognize the accents of Lord Merton and to realize that he was in a towering rage. What could have happened? She darted downstairs to see Merton wearing nothing but a white linen nightshirt. It came to his knees, revealing the bottom half of a pair of shapely legs.

She hesitated, wondering if she should go below when Lord Merton was so casually outfitted. In the end curiosity got the better of her and she continued down to the landing.

To her astonishment, Merton pointed a finger at her and roared, 'So you have managed to sneak back in despite my locking you out. By God, I cannot toss a lady out into the middle of the night as you deserve, but you shall leave here at first light, Miss Wainwright, and your father with you. I might have broken my neck!'

He moved his neck rather like a rooster, stretching it this way and that, to test that it was not broken. He uttered a yelp and put his palm to it, to ease the pain.

Charity felt the full odium of this unjustified attack. She stared haughtily and said, 'You need not wait until morning, milord. I shall leave at once, and my father with me. If you will be so kind as to call our carriage, Bagot.' She turned and began to stride upstairs with her head held high.

'Shall I call the doctor for you as well, milord?' Bagot asked uncertainly.

Merton limped to the bottom of the staircase and shouted at Charity, 'Get back down here at once.'

Lewis twitched at his brother's elbow. 'I say, John, that is a bit rough on Miss Wainwright.'

Miss Wainwright stopped, while her anger congealed to icy fury. She turned and slowly descended the staircase. 'I have not the slightest idea what you are talking about. I have not been out of the house, so I could hardly have *sneaked* back in. I heard your uncouth bellows and came to see if you required assistance. And I am not accustomed to being ordered about like a servant.'

'Are you saying you were not in my bedroom a moment ago?'

Her jaw fell. 'Milord! You go too far! Upon my word!'

Lewis scowled. 'I say, John! That is doing it a bit brown.'

Merton began to realize that Miss Wainwright had not had time to find some means back into the house, get upstairs to her

110

room, change her gown, and reappear so swiftly. In other words, he had made a flaming jackass of himself.

'Some woman was in my room,' he said, still angry.

'You may be very sure it was not I!' she said.

Bagot cleared his throat discreetly. 'Perhaps if your lordship would tell us exactly what happened? You will be more comfortable in the saloon,' he continued, taking Merton's elbow to guide him thither. 'A glass of wine would not go amiss. I shall give you a coat to put on, until I have time to run upstairs and get your dressing gown.'

In this calming manner he ushered Merton into the saloon, with a clearly discomfitted Lewis and an angry Miss Wainwright following behind. Bagot saw Merton to a sofa, lit a few lamps, and poured wine for the party. He then disappeared, to reappear a moment later carrying a long drab driving coat, which he arranged around Merton's shoulders, tucking the tail of it around his naked legs.

'Will you be requiring a doctor, your lordship?'

Merton did not wish to belittle the nature of his wounds. Being an invalid seemed his best hope of diminishing Miss Wainwright's wrath. On the other hand, he had no wish to have a sawbones poking about him.

'I daresay it can wait until morning, Bagot.'

Bagot was just leaving when Mr Wainwright

111

arrived. He had taken the time to don trousers and shirt and was just pulling his jacket into place when he entered.

'Was it Knagg?' he demanded, looking all around, perhaps hoping for a view of a ghost.

'Someone came into my room,' Merton said. 'A female—a light gown with a stain on the bodice.'

'The singing nun! I told you she was there,' Wainwright exclaimed joyously.

'It was no nun. It was a live female. I chased her downstairs. She left by the front door,' Merton informed him.

Wainwright glanced at the door, then back at the staircase. 'Would you have any objection to my having a word with her?'

'You are entirely welcome, but I fancy she is halfway to Eastleigh by now.'

'No, no. They never stray so far. I meant, may I go into your room, milord?'

Merton tossed up his hands in resignation. 'Why not? It is clear I am to get no sleep this night.'

Wainwright darted off, his eyes sparkling with anticipation.

Lewis said, 'You owe Miss Wainwright an apology, John.'

Merton turned as pink as a rose and turned to Charity. 'My head received a vicious bump. It was such an extraordinary thing, to awaken and see a strange woman approaching my bed.'

Charity was not appeased by this weak
112

excuse. 'I shall be happy to leave if I am not wanted here.'

'I want you,' Merton said angrily. The words hung pregnantly on the air as they exchanged a startled, almost embarrassed, look, then Charity looked swiftly away, her heart racing.

Lewis said, 'That ain't an apology, John.'

'I am aware of that,' Merton snapped. 'I am indeed sorry, Miss Wainwright. I pray you will ignore my ill-natured request that you leave.'

'It was not a request; it was an order,' she said. 'And to suggest that I was sneaking into your bedroom! Upon my word, I think I must leave, first thing in the morning.'

Merton risked a smile. 'This materialization of the singing nun will not encourage your papa to leave. '

Charity knew only too well this was true. As it seemed she must stay, she tossed her tousled curls and said, 'Well, it is very strange. Very likely it *was* the singing nun. '

'Ghosts do not leave the premises,' Merton said. 'We have your papa's word for it.'

'Do you think it might have been Miss Monteith?' Charity asked. She was sorry to let go of her pique so soon, but curiosity once more overcame her and she found it hard to be both angry and curious at the same time.

Merton had no such mixed feelings. He leaped on this idea like a dog on a bone. 'She was very annoyed with me when I ordered her out of Mama's room earlier this evening.

When I went to speak to Mama about Papa and Meg, you know.'

'Could the woman have been her, though?' Lewis asked. 'She is pretty ancient to be capering about the house at top speed.'

'It seemed like a young woman, which is why I thought Miss Wainwright...' Intercepting a gimlet stare from Charity, Merton spoke of other things. 'Unfortunately, I did not get a look at the face at all. She had a sort of mantle pulled low about it. She—or someone—had drawn my curtains. I saw her by moonlight. It was a frightening moment. I first thought it was the singing nun, but of course a second thought brought me to my senses.' He glanced at Lewis with the dawning of suspicion. Odd he was wearing his shoes and stockings.

'Old Monteith has got one of the servants to play this trick on you, depend on it,' Lewis said. 'Either that or it was the nun.'

'I shall question the servants tomorrow,' Merton said.

Lewis said doubtfully, 'I should not bother, John. It will only set them to cackling. Best to forget it. Unless it happens again, of course.'

Merton gave him a knowing look. 'You will see that it does not happen again, Lewis. I demmed near broke my neck.'

Lewis stared, the picture of innocence. 'What, are you suggesting I—'

'Cut bait. You were wide awake and waiting for my reaction. You bore no traces of sleep when you came bucketing downstairs. You ought to have at least mussed your hair and removed your shoes and stockings.'

Glancing at Lewis's feet, Charity noticed he was fully shod. 'So that is why you were absent after dinner, and why you wore that gloating look when you joined me later. Who was the ghost?' she demanded.

'I haven't the faintest idea what you are talking about,' Lewis said, trying to look offended.

But when Merton laughed, he said, 'Well, you deserved it. And now if you will excuse me, I ought to see that Millie gets home all right. Millie Dawson, old Ned Dawson's daughter. I set it up with her this afternoon, as she is always ripe for any rig.'

'Such rigs as this could put the pair of you on the gibbet,' Charity said. 'If Merton had broken his neck...'

Lewis rose and headed for the front door to check on Millie Dawson. 'You wasn't supposed to chase her, John. You was supposed to swoon. And you wasn't supposed to insult Miss Wainwright either,' he added as his parting shot.

'As to that,' Charity said nobly, 'Miss Wainwright is becoming accustomed to insults in this house.'

'She was not treated so badly at Radley Hall, I wager,' Merton said.

'No indeed. Nor at Beaulieu either.'

'And now I must cancel our ride tomorrow as well. I fear this ankle will keep me chairbound for a few days.'

'Oh, I knew we would not be riding,' she said. 'Papa told me not to pack my riding habit. He always knows.'

'Pity I went to the bother of sending a footman off to London for it.'

'Yes, I told you it was a waste of time, but some people do not listen to good advice. Would you like some assistance upstairs, milord? Shall I call Bagot, or will you require a brace of sturdy footmen?'

'Just put the wine decanter here beside me, if you will be so kind, and leave me to plot my revenge on Lewis. I shall not further aggravate the Wainwrights by interfering with your papa's ghost hunting in my chamber.'

'Don't be foolish. Of course you must go to bed if you are tired.'

'And my ankle aching like the devil, to say nothing of my wrenched neck.' He looked, hoping to see a sign of sympathy. Finding none, he added, 'And my wrenched pride.'

'You should have been forewarned, Merton. Did you not realize pride goeth before a fall? Talk about pride, what of mine? You were not ordered to leave the premises.'

He flicked a quizzical grin at her. 'I have not heard the last of that, have I?'

'No, sir. Not by a long chalk.'

'I shall have a rout party to repay you for

116

that infamous insult. Will that heal the breach?'

'I am very much inclined to forbid anything of the sort, but Papa told me to bring a special party frock, so there is no point. I shall leave you to your wine and your guilty conscience.' She rose, delivered the wine decanter, and glared. 'It is unbecoming behavior for you to smile in that *horrid* way when you should be feeling guilty,' she scolded.

'I am smiling to think how I shall make it up to you, Charity. No, no. You must not fly into a fresh pelter at my presumption in using your first name. I use it to remind you of your Christian duty. As the Good Book says, "Charity suffereth long, and is kind." '

'Yes, and charity begins at home. I shall have charity on myself and go back to bed. Good night, Merton.'

'Parting is such sweet sorrow.'

'*Au contraire.* Parting is a distinct pleasure, and I take leave to tell you, sir, you are no Romeo.' On this defiant speech she turned and left.

'I should hope not. Romeo was a young ass,' he called after her retreating figure.

The echo of a chuckle followed her as she went to the staircase. Once she was away from Merton, she allowed herself the luxury of a small, matching chuckle. How he had hated being caught in the wrong, making a fool of himself, and, most of all, apologizing. A few

117

more such blows and his pride might be battered down to size.

CHAPTER TEN

Despite his lame ankle, Merton was already at the breakfast table the next morning when Charity came downstairs. He and Lewis sat together, harmony restored after Lewis's prank. She was happy to see that Merton was not the kind of man who bore a grudge. He reached for the walking stick propped by his chair in a token effort of rising to greet her. Charity just smiled her sympathy and motioned him to remain seated. The smudges beneath his dark eyes told her he had not slept much.

'Good morning, Merton,' she said. 'You are not looking your usual hardy self. I hope the ankle did not give you too bad a night?'

'Good morning, Charity. I slept well enough once I got to bed—at three o'clock. The singing nun was extremely active in my chamber, according to Mr Wainwright. But she did not leave it. That was Lewis's little prank. It seems we had another haunting as well.'

'No!'

'Oh, yes. Or at least Mama is convinced it was a ghost.'

'But you nailed the attic window above her

118

room shut and blocked the holes in the clothespresses.'

'I fancy this ghost came directly from Miss Monteith's room.'

'It was a white pigeon,' Lewis said, looking up from his plate of gammon and eggs.

Merton swallowed his annoyance at having his story plundered, but continued. 'I heard Mama's shouts of terror as I was finally preparing for bed. I hobbled down the hallway to see what was amiss. When I opened the door, a bird flew into my face. It gave me the shock of my life, I can tell you. No wonder Mama was shrieking. She says it was the soul of Meg, come to haunt her. It is a vicious stunt to terrorize her,' he finished grimly.

'Could the bird have gotten in by an open window during the day and been awakened during the night?' she asked.

'That hardly seems likely. Pigeons are not insomniacs after all. Why should it sleep peacefully while she was in her room and awaken at two-thirty in the morning'

'Could have drugged it,' Lewis suggested. 'Fed it a mouthful of laudanum.'

Charity nodded. 'Papa has felt from the first that Miss Monteith should be let go.'

'Easier said than done, unfortunately,' Merton replied. 'Mama has become attached to her. Something else occurs to me as well. This latest "haunting" happened just after Mama spoke to Penley about giving that five thousand to the charity fund. She had not definitely decided to do it.'

'*My* five thousand,' Lewis muttered.

'You are suggesting some connivance between St John and Miss Monteith?' Charity asked.

'Not necessarily. My thinking is that Miss Monteith is after the money for herself. She wishes to convince Mama to give the money to her, not the fund. She is Meg's sister after all, her closest living relative. A sort of posthumous bequest.'

'Did your mama mention this possibility?'

'No, she was too upset to talk rationally. Miss Monteith gave her a paregoric draft. And suggested that Mama would like to move to another room—now that we have made her own chamber ghost-proof'

'I see! Do you know which room? We should have a close look at it.'

'No, I shall discover that later today. But enough of this lugubrious talk. I am sorry we must miss our ride, as it is such a fine day. I had been looking forward to it.'

Charity saw no reason why a sore leg need keep them from a drive in his carriage, but Lord Merton did not suggest that alternative.

'I shall manage to amuse myself,' she said. 'I shall go to take a look at Meg Monteith's grave. Shall I take flowers, as you mentioned doing last night?'

Merton had been envisaging a quiet

morning with Charity, perhaps in the solarium or sitting in the garden, talking. It was her insouciant mention of doing other things that brought the frown to his brow. Before he could answer her question regarding the flowers, Lewis spoke up.

'I shall show you the grave, Miss Wainwright. And a few other points of interest as well. Did John tell you we have our own hermit? And a grotto and all.'

'A hermit!' Charity exclaimed. 'How very odd!'

'Did Radley Hall not have a hermit, ma'am?' Merton inquired satirically.

'No, but they had a lovely chapel.'

'We have a chapel, too,' Lewis boasted. 'If you can call it a chapel. It looks like a big barn inside. Cromwell's lads ripped out all the stained glass and pictures and statues. It is nothing but a bare white-washed room now.'

'It is considered the best example of its sort in England!' Merton felt obliged to mention it. 'Most of the others have been semirestored to their former glory. Ours is perfectly intact, an outstanding example of the period.'

'That is John's excuse for not restoring it as it used to be,' Lewis explained. 'Our stable is fancier than our chapel.'

'We have historical societies touring it on a regular basis, begging me not to tamper with it,' Merton said.

'Truth to tell, we Mertons were never much

121

for religion,' Lewis added, to give the true explanation for the chapel's Puritan austerity.

Charity said without much enthusiasm, 'I should like to see it.'

'Eat up, then, and we shall be off. Pity you cannot come with us, John. Would you like me to haul you to your office before we leave?' Lewis asked.

'I can manage, thank you. I plan to take a book of poetry out to the garden.'

Lewis stared as if looking at a zebra or some other exotic animal at the Exeter Exchange. 'Poetry! By Jove, you ought to get that bump on your head looked at. You never read poetry. I shall fetch you the *Farmers' Monthly* before I leave. Are you nearly finished, Miss Wainwright?'

'No, I have just begun,' she replied, and continued eating her toast and eggs. 'What poetry will you read, Merton?' she inquired. 'Do you read the older poets or Byron?'

He hesitated a moment, not wanting to appear stuffy but uncertain as to whether she might find Byron fast.

'John has never bought a book of poems in his life,' Lewis told her. 'If he has gone soft in the head in his old age, he is reading ancient stuff from the library. I doubt he has ever heard of Byron.'

'I happen to be a friend and admirer of Byron!' Merton objected. When this failed to impress his guest, he added, 'I shall probably

122

have another look at Southey this morning, however.' This brought no reaction from Charity. 'What poets do you admire, Charity?' he asked.

'I do not read much poetry,' she said. 'I prefer novels. I like something to happen in books I am reading—a story, you know, and not just descriptions of flowers and things.'

'I could not agree with you more,' Lewis said at once, robbing Merton of the opportunity to agree. 'But Byron gives you a dandy story as well as the trees and oceans and all. He is keen on oceans. You really ought to give him a try, Miss ... Charity,' he said with a bold look at Merton. That look said, If you can call her Charity, so can I.

'It does not seem like a story when everything rhymes, though, does it?' she said.

Lewis frowned importantly and replied, 'There is something in that, by Jove. I have just been thumbing through Fanny Burney's latest offering.' He hadn't, but his mama had a copy that he could lend Miss Wainwright if she wanted a novel.

'I love Fanny Burney!' Charity exclaimed. 'And Maria Edgeworth and Mrs Radcliffe.'

'By the living jingo, we are as like as peas in a pod. Let us go to the graveyard.' Charity had now finished her breakfast. She rose, said good-bye to Merton, then they left, chatting about books.

'I shall show you the library later. And this

afternoon we shall...' Merton heard his brother's voice fade out as Lewis walked off with Charity. She was supposed to be riding with him this morning, stopping by the stream to enjoy the bluebells. And instead he sat alone, with his demmed ankle throbbing like a bad tooth.

When the footman came to refill his cup, he said, 'Send for the sawbones. I want to get this ankle strapped up to allow me to walk. And ride.'

'Yes, milord.'

While Merton suffered the discomfort of having a doctor poke at his swollen ankle, Lewis and Charity went to the family graveyard. It was a perfect spring day, with the sun sending down shafts of light to fur the treetops with gold. The small family plot was hedged in by wild thornbushes, with yews along one side. Wildflowers grew between the ancient gravestones, bringing a touch of life to the place of death. Impressive marble angels and crosses marked the last resting places of the lords of Merton, with lesser stones to mark the graves of younger sons and daughters.

'That is the church,' Lewis said, pointing to a squat gray stone building in the Norman style. 'The little half-timbered cottage beside it is the vicarage, where St John lives. Meg is planted over there,' he added, pointing to the very edge of the burial yard. 'She don't have a monument. There is a little plaque lying flat on the ground. Odd she was buried here at all, but I daresay it is because of her son. I mean to say, if he was Papa's son, then that might account for it. They are supposed to be buried together, in the one grave.'

They found the simple stone. It read: Margaret Elizabeth Monteith, 1767–1784, and newly born son, Roger. 'She was only seventeen when she died,' Charity said softly. 'So young, her life hardly begun.'

'To say nothing of Roger,' Lewis added. 'There is an odd story about this grave. I had it of Muffal, the poacher. He says there is no kid in the grave.' Charity frowned. 'How would he know? Surely a poacher did not see the open coffin.'

'P'raps he dug up the ground and opened the coffin, but more likely he had the story of whoever put Meg in her box. Anyhow, Muffal told me the tale when I was a lad. I never forgot it.'

'But if that is true, then perhaps Meg never had a child at all.'

'Of course she did. It has having the child that killed her.'

'Was it?' Charity asked, and stared at him until he grasped her meaning. 'Or was it a pretext for murder?'

'Good lord! Are you suggesting Mama had her done away with?'

'I don't know. I believe I am.'

'Rubbish. John talked to Mama. She told

him Meg was big as a barrel. And she could not have stuffed herself with a cushion, for Papa would certainly have known the difference.'

'Not if he had stopped—I mean to say, once your Mama returned from her visit, he probably stopped seeing Meg—privately.'

'Without her shift on, you mean,' Lewis said. 'Yes, I see what you are getting at. It was all a trick to con money out of Papa. But they would have had to come up with a child eventually. I daresay Muffal was talking through his hat, trying to frighten me.'

'Is this poacher still around?'

'Of course he is. I could have a go at him. Daresay he will deny the whole thing, but I remember very well what he told me. A blasphemy, he called it. I half expected a bolt of lightning to rip down from the sky and rend the grave asunder.'

'Where could we find him?'

'In the spinney after dark, but it would be as much as your life is worth to go after him. He would take the noise of our approach for a rabbit and blow our heads—er, feet off.'

'He must be somewhere during the day.'

'He has a little shack down by the stream. I don't know why John lets him stay, for the fellow lives off our rabbits and pheasants. Mind you, he is an excellent hand at ridding the park of moles, and he got rid of the rats in the cellar at home a while back. Does a bit of rat catching hereabouts.'

'Let us visit him.'

'If you like. I daresay John will ring a peal over me for taking you to meet Muffal. He drinks, you see. His shack is this way. He should not be bottled yet at this hour.'

He led Charity from the graveyard, across a meadow to the stream. 'We could have ridden if I'd known we were going this far. I wanted to show you our hermit. He won't talk to you. He gave it up. Talking, I mean. He lives in a cave. God only knows how he survives.'

'I believe it is the custom for the mistress of the estate to provide the hermit with meals in return for his prayers for the family's well being,' Charity explained. 'He also acts as a sort of religious consultant.'

'A regular take-in,' Lewis said. 'We must do his laundry as well. I always wondered how he keeps his robe so clean. He wears white. As to praying, it is St John who will pray us all into heaven. He lives in Mama's pocket.'

They came to a row of willows, trailing their branches into the stream. 'There is where Muffal lives,' Lewis said, pointing to a shack that tilted precariously to the left. It was about ten feet square, built of unpainted boards, with a tar-paper roof. Three dead hares hung in the unglazed window.

'It must be cold in winter,' Charity said, staring at the horrible domicile.

'Muffal goes to the poorhouse in Eastleigh in the winter. This is his summer residence. He

127

will be fishing, I expect. You would be surprised how big some of the fish in this stream are.' He cupped his mouth with his hands and shouted, 'Halloo. It's Winton, Muffal. Are you home?' Aside to Charity he added, 'I would not take you into the place for a wilderness of monkeys. I don't know how he can stand the stench of rotting meat and dead fish.' This said, he cupped his hands and shouted again.

Almost immediately, a bearded, filthy man dressed in a ragged grogram coat of ancient vintage, with a misshapen beaver hat pulled low over his eyes, appeared around the corner. In his right hand he held a fishing rod.

'G'day, melord.' He grinned, revealing a few shattered remains of teeth. 'They be biting t'day.'

'G'day, Muffal. I want to ask you something.' He went a little closer, with Charity hanging somewhat behind. 'Do you mind telling me some years ago about Meg Monteith's grave?'

'Aye, Meg and the wee one.'

'You said there was no baby buried with her. The gravestone says there is.'

'Stones can lie as well as folks, I'm thinking.'

'So you are saying Meg is alone in that grave?'

'Meg and the worms. That's all, melord.'

'How do you come to know that?'

'Why, 'tis well known as an old ballad. Meg

128

sleeps alone, for t'first time since her put up her hair and let down her skirts. Hee hee.'

'Yes, but how do you know? Who told you? Or did you see her being put in the coffin?'

Muffal lifted his hat and scratched his hair. ''Twas that long ago I don't rightly remember, but I know Meg sleeps alone. Ah, she were a bonnie lass.'

Charity nudged Lewis's elbow and whispered, 'Ask him if she was ever *enceinte*.'

Lewis went a few steps closer and said, 'Are you sure Meg ever had a babe at all, Muffal?'

'That she had, to judge by the yelling and screaming that night. I mind it well. We all see'd her body swelling day by day.'

'Where did she give birth to this baby, then?' Lewis asked.

'If you're wanting to know more, 'tis Old Ned you mun talk to. Ned knows more than he says.'

'You mean the hermit?' Lewis asked.

'Aye, Ned Carbury that was, afore he took religion. A fine toper was Ned, but the books destroyed him. He were always a lad for book reading. Ah, there was weird and wild goings-on in them days. Ned was groom at the big house, courting Meg, afore she caught His Lordship's eye. He got elevated pretty quick to post of hermit with all its perkizzits.'

A rabbit darted through the meadow. Muffal dropped his fishing line. 'Be that all, melord? There is a fine hopper waiting for my

129

jiggle bag.'

Lewis could think of nothing more to ask and let Muffal go. As he walked away with Charity, he said, 'I told you. There is no baby buried in that grave. Never was, never will be.'

'I wonder if Muffal learned it from Ned, the hermit. We should speak to him.'

'Ned don't talk. That is the sort of hermit he is. He just prays, and on fine days he might sit in the sun and read for a spell.'

She directed a meaningful look at Lewis. 'Very convenient, his taking a vow of silence.'

'I don't know that it is a vow. Ned never actually took holy orders. He is a sort of amateur holy man.'

'He was given this sinecure of hermit by your father to pay him off for losing Meg.'

'I fancy that was the way of it. A pretty slim reward it was, too, but then if he had a taste for books...'

'We have got to talk to Ned,' Charity said.

CHAPTER ELEVEN

Charity looked around, wondering where the grotto might be. Other than the graveyard, there was nothing but natural beauty around her. The meadows, the park, the stream.

'The grotto is this way,' Lewis said, pointing off to the far side of the estate. 'We walked westward; the grotto is to the east.'

As they passed behind the Hall, Charity glanced up to admire the soaring stone walls and pointed windows. It was difficult to be certain, with the sun shining in her eyes, but she thought she noticed a head at one of the bedroom windows.

'Whose window is that?' she asked, pointing it out to Lewis.

'That is the east wing. Only Mama and Miss Monteith are using it at the moment. Mama had thought of putting you there, since you are a girl and John and I sleep in the west wing, but as your papa was along, she decided there was no impropriety in letting you have the Queen Elizabeth Suite after all.'

'Someone was watching us,' she said. The Hall was built on the summit of a small incline. Whoever had been watching would have had a view of the graveyard and perhaps even of Muffal's shack. At least she (of course it was Miss Monteith she feared was watching) would have seen the direction they had gone in.

'Daresay it was John. He hobbled upstairs to keep an eye on us. I noticed he has taken to calling you Charity. Not like him. Sorry I called you Charity at breakfast. I only did it to rag John. He is usually stiff as a poker with guests Mama imports against his will. You want to be careful, Miss Wainwright, or he will be pestering you with an offer.'

'Oh, I do not think that at all likely,' Charity

131

replied, biting back a smile. 'After the scold he gave me last night, it is more likely to be an order to get out than an offer of marriage.'

'He felt demmed foolish about that. Serves him right to make a cake of himself. He is too toplofty by half. I only did it for a lark. How was I to know the gudgeon would take off after Millie and bust his ankle? But that is always the way, ain't it? You only want a bit of fun and end up in the suds. There is the chapel. Do you want to take a peek?'

They did just that; took one quick peek at the Spartan room before continuing on their way. It seemed a great pity to Charity that the lovely little Gothic chapel, so pretty on the outside, had been stripped of all its ornaments within.

'Ned lives in the woods yonder,' Lewis said, pointing to a stand of ancient oaks with a path leading through it. 'You might see him sunning himself at the edge of the stream. It winds through the woods. I catch a glimpse of him from time to time when I am out riding. He usually has his nose in a book, but sometimes he is just sitting there. He might be asleep, to judge by the looks of him, but as he is a holy man I daresay he is thinking of how many angels can dance on the head of a pin or some such deep thing.'

They continued for about a quarter of a mile through the woods. The air was cool and moist, with tall branches filtering the sun that came in sudden shafts of glory between the trees to light patches of wildflowers. The uneven path was slippery underfoot from last autumn's fallen leaves. Squirrels chased one another up the tree trunks, chattering busily. Overhead, a jackdaw croaked a warning of their approach to the woods' unsuspecting inhabitants. When they came to the stream, Lewis veered off the path and continued for about two hundred yards.

'There it is,' he said, pointing to a little stone grotto built into the side of a hill.

There were no statues or any indication that the grotto was used at all. It was shallow, with a squirrel scuttling through the grass.

'He cannot live there!' Charity exclaimed. 'Where is his cave?'

'It ain't a cave, exactly, but somehow we always speak of the hermit as living in a cave. Seems more hermitlike. His house is just there, beside the grotto. It seemed the proper place to put him. Hermits and grottos go together like gammon and mustard.'

She looked and discovered a pretty stone cottage set off a few yards from the grotto. It was small, perhaps comprising two rooms on one floor. It looked snug and modern, more like a tenant's cottage than a hermit's nook.

'Papa built it for him. I shall give the door a rap and see if he is about.'

So saying, he approached the door and tapped. They waited; Lewis tapped again. No sound came from within. He tried the door and found it locked.

'It is strange he would lock his door when he is in such an isolated place,' Charity said.

'Poachers. Muffal would steal the fleas off a dog. We shall try the stream' was his next idea.

There, sunning himself on a large rock, sat the hermit. He had long white hair and a severe face, with some suggestion of a marble monument in its austerity. The face was not white, however, but well tanned, with a pair of startling blue eyes set deep on either side of a prominent nose. His robe was snowy white. A staff like a shepherd's crook sat on the ground beside the rock.

'I say, Ned,' Lewis called, walking forward.

The hermit leaped up as if he had been shot at. What struck Charity was the man's fierce eyes. At this close range she saw that they were shockingly bloodshot.

'Hence home, you idle creatures!' he exclaimed, pointing toward the Hall and looking like Jehovah in a very bad temper.

'I just want to ask you a question,' Lewis said. The hermit examined him suspiciously. 'About Meg Monteith and her child.'

The hermit said no more. He rose from his rock, picked up his staff, and marched stiffly off to his pleasant-looking little cottage. From that impressive visage Charity had expected a tall, gaunt frame, but the hermit was short and slight.

Lewis shrugged. 'I told you he wouldn't talk. A regular statue. There is no point following him.'

'He did speak. He quoted Shakespeare. That is odd, is it not?'

'Eh? What are you talking about?'

'That "home, you idle creatures!" That is Shakespeare. From *Julius Caesar*, I think. I would have expected something from the Bible.'

'I never can tell them apart. Very likely Ned can't either.'

'But where would he have come across Shakespeare? He was only a groom before he became a hermit. One assumes his reading since then would be of sermons and holy writing. Did you notice his eyes were very bloodshot?'

'No doubt he was up praying half the night, or studying, or flagellating himself, or doing whatever it is hermits do.'

'Or drinking,' Charity said, though it was possible a late night of reading might have caused those red eyes.

They returned, retracing their steps through the pretty forest without incident. When they reached the Hall, they found Merton in the Blue Saloon waiting for them, with his bandaged ankle propped up on a footstool. The bandage had required the removal of one topboot, which had been replaced by a patent evening slipper. He hastily picked up the book

135

of poetry he had laid aside an hour before in favor of the *Farmer's Monthly*.

'You missed all the excitement,' Merton said. 'We have had a visit from Knagg despite the locked door and sealed windows. Why, it is enough to make a man believe in ghosts.'

'Especially if he wants to ingratiate Miss Wainwright's papa,' Lewis added, grinning from ear to ear.

Charity appeared unmoved by both Merton's announcement and Lewis's gibe. 'Has Papa sorted out the relationship between Knagg and Walter yet?'

'They are half brothers; they have the same mama,' Merton told her. 'Knagg's papa was for king and country, and Knagg followed in his father's footsteps. Walter, né Charles, was the son of one of Cromwell's men. The half brothers met, and died in battle, here at Keefer Hall, but they did not kill each other.'

'And the singing nun?' Charity asked. 'Papa mentioned the possibility of a connection between the three of them.'

They were neighbors, all local folks. That is the only connection. He is upstairs with the singing nun now, attempting to discover her tale. It should be amusing to learn what she was doing in a monk's cell. But enough of that. What have you two been up to?'

'Miss Wainwright thinks Mama murdered Meg,' Lewis said.

'Does she indeed!' Merton replied with an

136

astonished look. 'Is there no end to Miss Wainwright's inventiveness? My being a bastard is not enough for you?' he asked, damping down his anger. 'Now you label Mama a murderess!'

'I merely suggested it as one possibility among many,' she explained dismissingly.

'Because of there not being a child in Meg's grave, you see,' Lewis explained.

'That is news to me!' Merton said. 'Surely the gravestone indicates a double burial.'

'Told her it was no such thing,' Lewis said. 'About Mama, I mean. As to the grave, she is dead right. Did Muffal never tell you the story, John?' he asked, amazed at such a lack of initiative on his brother's part.

'I do not number Muffal among my confidants,' Merton said dampingly.

'You ought to. He is a mine of information. I have known forever that Meg was alone in that grave. Old Ned, the hermit, could confirm it if he would, but you know Ned. He will never say a word.'

'Except to quote Shakespeare,' Charity added. 'And furthermore I think he drinks more than is good for him. His eyes were as red as radishes.'

'You should not have disturbed Ned, Lewis,' Merton chided. 'Our hermit is not a mere ornament to amuse our guests, as some are. He is a genuine holy man.'

Lewis accepted this without arguing. 'Did

you know Papa gave him the post of hermit when he stole Meg Monteith from him?'

'More of old Muffal's imaginings?' Merton asked, cocking an eyebrow in derision.

'I had the story from Muffal,' Lewis admitted.

'Muffal is a nasty piece of mischief. I wish you would not speak to him.'

Charity asked, 'Why do you allow him to live on the estate if you dislike his character, Merton?'

'Why, he has lived here forever.'

She knew this was always sufficient reason for continuing a pointless or even dangerous tradition in the noble homes of England. At Beaulieu Lord Montagu harbored a known felon, who had a knack for devising superior fish lures.

'Besides,' Merton added, 'he does an excellent job of keeping the park free of moles.'

'He is a demmed fine rat catcher as well,' Lewis added. 'Cleared out our cellar in one afternoon. I say, John, is the Armaments Room open now? I should like to have a look-in to see how Knagg is behaving.'

'Yes, it is open. I have allowed Mr Wainwright to put the offending objects away in a chest in a corner of the room. If that does not satisfy Knagg, I may have them removed to another room.'

'Don't take them to your own bedchamber,' Lewis advised. 'I mean to say, the nun would not want them near her. She must have been dead set against Cromwell, eh? Her being a nun and him destroying our chapel.'

He left, and Charity took his seat closer to Merton. He prepared a smile, looking forward to some private conversation of an intimate sort.

She said, 'Someone upstairs was watching us from the east wing. Miss Monteith, I daresay.'

'That is possible. I am sorry I missed our ride this morning. I was particularly looking forward to it.'

'Yes,' she said impatiently. 'I daresay Miss Monteith is upstairs?'

'I have not seen her down here. I believe, now that I have had my ankle tended to, I may be able to ride tomorrow.'

'No, we will not be riding. I should have listened to Papa. Where is your mama, Merton?'

Merton saw there was to be no romance until he had discussed the apparition at the window. 'St John is with her at the moment, consoling her for last night's invasion by the pigeon. I mean to move Mama to another room before nightfall. I am convinced Monteith introduced that bird into her chamber. It is enough to put me in charity with St John. Better he should get Mama's money than that Monteith should. I have invited him to take lunch with us. I shall sound him out on his plans for the fund. If I approve, I shall not

139

try to dissuade Mama from giving him half her fortune.'

As Merton was alone, Charity thought it polite to spend a little time with him during his convalescence. Glancing about, she noticed the book of poetry on the table and said, 'I see you have been indulging your taste for poetry, Merton. That surprises me. I would not have taken you for the poetic sort.'

He studied this for either insult or praise. As he had no use whatever for poetry, and as Charity had claimed a lack of interest equal to his own, he decided it was no insult at least.

'It helps to pass an idle hour on such occasions as this, when I am chairbound.' He proceeded to put the opening to more personal use. 'Er, what sort do you take me for, Charity?'

'A very practical, down-to-earth gentleman. Keefer Hall appears so prosperous that you are obviously a good manager.'

This, while hardly romantic, was one sort of praise to please Merton. He was proud of his estate management. Had she been a gentleman, this discussion might have continued into the byways of sheep rearing and crop rotation. As she was an attractive young lady, he said only, 'I am considered a fair manager, I believe.'

'It is generally the way with you unimaginative gentlemen,' she said unthinkingly.

140

Merton's jaw moved silently. 'What is your reading of yourself? What sort of young lady are you? I would have thought one of your highly imaginative faculties would be a lover of poetry.'

'No, by and large I find it silly. I like flowers, but to turn them into sentient beings goes too far for me. I am really very boring,' she replied blandly. 'I am not poetical or artistic or musical. I do not know what I am precisely. Since I began to grow up, I have never been in one place long enough to find out. I cannot even make up my mind as to whether I believe in ghosts. Papa does seem to have some unexplained power.'

'I believe it is the power of hindsight. He can explain matters after the fact. For instance, we Dechastelaines have always been loyalists. My Armaments Room holds mostly artifacts from wars defending the monarchy. That little yellow jerkin and the round helmet are obviously out of place there. Hence your papa has decided they are the cause of the mischief. It is but a short step to claim that a Cromwellian spirit is doing the mischief'

'Ye-e-e-s-s,' she agreed reluctantly. 'But the table *was* overturned when the room was sealed and locked. Over the years there have been other occurrences in other houses we have visited. I keep an open mind.'

'When I see a real ghost, then I shall open my mind a little. Meanwhile I am a disbeliever. In
141

the interest of making your papa's visit peaceful, however, I am willing to pretend to suspend my disbelief'

'A hypocrite, in fact,' she said, when he was only trying to be polite.

Before he could retaliate, Lewis came pelting into the room. His face was paper-white. 'I say, John! Did you not tell me you had put the jerkin and the helmet in that little chest?'

'Yes, I put them there myself. Why—'

'Because they are back on the table. And Bagot assures me no one went near the Armaments Room. Mr Wainwright is upstairs in his chamber, so you cannot say he did it for a trick.'

'Well, I'll be damned!' Merton exclaimed, and grabbed his walking stick to hoist himself out of his chair.

Charity cocked her head at him. 'Is your mind beginning to open a crack yet, Merton?' She laughed.

They heard a crash from the Armaments Room as they hastened toward it. By the time they reached it, the yellow jerkin and the helmet had been flung to the floor once more.

'I must tell Papa!' Charity exclaimed, and ran off after him.

Merton stared at the offending articles. There was no point blaming Lewis for this. He might have removed the articles from the trunk and put them on the table. He had certainly not knocked them off. He had not been near the room when that happened.

When Lewis went to pick the things up, Merton said, 'Leave them there. We shall let Wainwright handle this. I am beginning to think there are more things on earth than are dreamt of in my philosophy.'

'Very likely,' Lewis agreed, 'since you never had any philosophy so far as I have seen.'

CHAPTER TWELVE

Mr Wainwright was chirping merry at lunch, with the exciting goings-on in the Armaments Room.

'Now that I know the relationship between Knagg and Walter, I shall go through the papers in the library in an effort to prove what they told me. Actually it was Knagg who spoke to me. He is the stronger presence. He is three years older than Walter, who is the son by the second marriage, you see. Knagg's father was a knight attached to Baron Merton—known as Baron Dechastelaine in those days. Walter's papa was not so highly placed in society. There may be no mention of him in the documents, but with luck perhaps there will be a line somewhere of a knight's lady remarrying upon the death of her husband. It is surprising the amount of detail that was written down in the old days.'

143

Lady Merton listened to all this with impatience, then said, 'You have not been to my chamber to investigate what happened last night, Mr Wainwright.'

'I have never heard of a soul returning in the form of a bird,' he said comprehensively. 'I can only say that if it is so, then the fact that the bird is white suggests it is a shriven soul, an innocent and not a malign spirit. Would you not agree, St John?'

The vicar cleared his throat and replied, 'Just so, but surely you are forgetting one ghost that comes in the form of a bird, Wainwright. I refer, of course, to the Holy Ghost, the third person of the Trinity who is usually symbolized as a white dove.'

'Are you saying the Holy Ghost entered my room?' Lady Merton exclaimed, turning stark-white herself and trembling in fright.

'My dear lady, nothing of the sort, I assure you,' St John said. 'A glass of wine for her ladyship,' he called to the footman, who hastened forward to fill her glass.

Merton could take no more. 'This is demmed nonsense!' he scoffed. 'As if ghosts weren't bad enough, now you are speaking of divine apparitions, the Holy Ghost flying about in the dark. It is a sacrilege.'

St John clasped his hands, as if about to pray. 'That was an unfortunate misunderstanding, milord. I meant nothing of the sort. It was a mere academic discussion. To speak of ordinary ghosts as being a sacrilege, however, is inaccurate. Why, the ghost of Jesus Christ came to Doubting Thomas, if you will recall. To say nothing of Samuel, as I mentioned the other day. I have no doubt her ladyship was visited by a ghost, an innocent, harmless ghost.'

Merton just glared. 'I trust you will not preach this sort of balderdash from the pulpit, Reverend.'

'I agree it is best not to excite uneducated minds by speaking of such things. They would surely misunderstand, but that is not to say that among ourselves we need ignore the obvious.'

'It seems to me that is exactly what we are doing,' Merton said. 'A pigeon got into Mama's room—by some as yet undetermined means,' he added, staring at Miss Monteith, who ignored him. She seldom took any part in the conversation at table.

Wainwright frowned. 'You do not have a dovecote at the Hall, though. I have not seen any pigeons about at all. I daresay it is the ravens on the roof that keep them at bay. They can be pesky things, pigeons.'

'There is no shortage of pigeons in the neighborhood. I mean to remove Mama to the west wing tonight and check her room carefully before she retires. I suggest you lock your door as well, Mama. We shall see if this pigeon is capable of passing through a locked door.'

'I shall do it, just to prove to you that the bird is a ghost,' Lady Merton replied, with a stubborn thrust of her chin.

Lewis chose that moment, when the matter seemed settled, to introduce his penny's worth. 'Seems to me a bird would be the perfect embodiment for a ghost. I mean to say, it could scoot right down from heaven, having wings and all. You ought to have your society look into it, Mr Wainwright. And about there not being any other bird ghosts, I fear you are out there. You are forgetting Coleridge's *Ancient Mariner*. What else was the albatross but a ghost, when you come down to it?'

'It has been transmogried from a symbol, has it?' Merton asked with a fierce stare.

'I may have misread it. Coleridge is very deep. I shall have another glance at it after lunch.'

'I suggest you leave off poetry,' Merton said. 'There is such a thing as being overly imaginative.' He directed a scowl along the board to Miss Wainwright at this speech.

Charity found lunch a positive ordeal. Merton did everything but call Miss Monteith a crook and St John a quack. To compound the offense, he paid no attention whatever to herself except for that one scowl.

Merton was aware that he was behaving atrociously, but he could not seem to stop himself. Try as he might, he could come up

146

with no sane explanation for the activity in the Armaments Room. To suddenly have to consider the possibility that ghosts were real phenomena was enough to upset his equilibrium.

Whatever of Knagg and Walter, he did not believe that the bird in his mama's room had been a ghost any more than he believed the singing nun had serenaded him that night. There was more chicanery than haunting in the business, and he felt in his bones that his mama's fortune was at the bottom of it. He was a man who liked to take charge, to handle things. Mama's insistence on keeping Miss Monteith tied to her apron strings made it impossible, resulting in great frustration for him.

He meant to pacify St John before he left, however, and so invited him into his study to discuss the St Alban's fund.

'Mama has told me of her notion of making over half her fortune to the fund,' he said. 'I would like to know more of your plans for the money.'

St John regarded Merton suspiciously. 'I consider it an emergency fund, milord, to assist the needy of the parish. Just this week I donated fifty pounds to the Halperins. They are not on your estate. Halperin is a clerk. He works in Eastleigh but lives in that little cottage near my vicarage. He needs his mount to get to work. It died last week, of old age. How could he support his family if he could not get to work? He has five children. It seemed the charitable thing to do.'

'Of course.'

'He knew a fellow who would sell him a decent nag for fifty pounds. The bank would not lend him the money, for his house is already mortgaged. There was another offer on the mount. It is such emergencies as this that make the fund so valuable. I might say necessary.'

'I agree in principle, but five thousand pounds is a great deal of money to set aside for such trifling emergencies.'

'It would be earning interest in the meanwhile. I am a strict watcher of pennies, milord. You need not fear I shall squander the money. I hope to use it for scholarships as well. Occasionally a bright child comes along. It seems a shame if he is not allowed to further his education, to be in a position to help his family, keep them off the dole,' he added, as this would naturally be of interest to a rate payer.

'I, myself, received my education as a result of the late Lord Merton's generosity. Had it not been for that, and your own generosity in giving me the living of St Alban's, I might have ended up a common laborer. I know better than most the value of charity, the difference a little money can make to a struggling youngster.'

Merton soon lost interest; he had heard this

tale before. He had no doubt of St John's honesty and sincerity. He rather felt some big project should be undertaken with such a large sum, but meanwhile he had other nagging concerns. Even as he sat there, listening to St John prose on, Charity might be making some plans with Lewis, and he wished to include himself in them if possible.

'We shall speak of it another time,' he said, rising from behind his desk. 'Just one more word: I wish you would not encourage Mama in this ghost business.'

St John clapped a white hand to his forehead. 'I could have bitten my tongue off when I realized how she misinterpreted my remark about the Holy Ghost! Most unfortunate. And about my sermons, you need have no fear that I mean to excite the common folks by any preaching of that sort. Indeed I do not belabor the point with her ladyship. I merely listen to her and offer such poor consolation as my reading of Holy Scripture suggests to me.'

While St John spoke, Merton nudged him toward the door. 'Very good of you,' he said, opening the door and peering down the hall to look for Charity.

The vicar left, and Merton limped after him toward the Blue Saloon. He found Lewis but not Charity.

'Where is Miss Wainwright?' he asked.

'She is with her papa in the library, going

through old documents to look for a trace of Walter.'

'As I am unable to ride, you might make a tour of the estate for me, Lewis, to see that all is going well.'

'What am I to look for?' Lewis asked in confusion.

'Sick sheep. Mildewed or withered or shrunken corn. Blight, undue water in the barley field. I fear I may have to have it tiled. These are the things you should be taking an interest in, not taking Miss Wainwright to visit poachers and hermits.'

Lewis rose reluctantly. 'Do you think Meg was murdered, John?' he asked.

'Don't be ridiculous.'

'But if there is no baby in the grave...'

'I cannot imagine why you choose to listen to the ravings of that drunken poacher. The child is buried with Meg. It was a boy named Roger. If necessary, I could have the grave dug up to prove it.'

'Did you learn anything from St John? Has he talked Mama out of my money?'

'I fear you have lost five thousand. Console yourself that it will go for good causes. St John tells me he gave fifty pounds to Halperin recently to buy a nag. There is no reason to doubt him.'

'It is true. I heard Halperin's nag had died of old age, and I saw him on that bay gelding Jim Henderson was trying to sell.' Lewis stood, frowning.

'Then what troubles you?'

'It is just that ... Well, I thought you was the treasurer of the fund. Can St John sign checks without you knowing about it?'

'He does not bother me with such trifling sums. Naturally I would be involved if any major expenditure were contemplated. St John hasn't the imagination to contemplate anything on a grand scale, however.'

'Then I wonder why he is so eager to get his hands on my five thousand,' Lewis said, and left.

*　　　*　　　*

In the library Wainwright had placed a wooden chest bound in brass on the table and was up to his elbows in dusty papers from the days of Cromwell. Charity spotted a small sheaf of papers consisting of yellowing pages, held together by faded blue ribbons. This suggested to her a lady's diary or common book. She lifted it up to examine it. The ink was hardly darker than the discolored papers, but the writing was legible. 'Diary of Margaret Dechastelaine' was written on the title page. Charity took it to the window for better light and began browsing through it, stumbling over the unaccustomed spellings and archaic words.

The lady had written of her daily doings. Charity judged from the confused writing style

151

that Margaret was a young girl. Such simple things as fashioning herself a new green mantle and gathering flowers in the meadow rested on the same page as preparing for the invasion of the Roundheads. She wrote of eating with tin forks, as the silverplate had been buried to keep it from the invaders. This did not prevent the family from entertaining guests at dinner, however. 'Seventeen guests to dinner, none of them of much interest.'

Halfway through the book, Margaret and several other local ladies had removed to a house identified only as Aunt Mary's home, taking some of the family jewels, valuable paintings, and small statues. Among the ladies who made the move was a Dame Sydwell, widow, included despite her late husband's and son's desertions to Cromwell's cause 'for Dame Sydwell's two brothers and her elder son, Knagg, are such brave Cavaliers, and much trusted by Papa.' The name Knagg leaped off the page.

Charity read on eagerly. News of the invasion came secondhand to Aunt Mary's from Keefer Hall. 'Heavy losses suffered; twenty-nine of Papa's men killed, eleven injured, but the estate still in our hands.' Wounded Cavaliers were brought to Aunt Mary's for treatment. 'The Duchene brothers both maimed, one lost an arm, the other an eye. Supplies are running low. The stench of blood and death in the great hall is intolerable.

I did not get but three hours sleep last night, and that a nightmare. But I must not complain; Papa still lives.'

Charity stopped reading to rest her eyes from the faded, spidery script. What an experience for a young girl! To be pitched from a life of luxury to such horrors as this. There was not even a doctor at the makeshift hospital. The care of the wounded fell entirely on the ladies. Charity read on. And in the midst of it all someone called Mrs Littlemore was delivered of a child 'at ten of the morning. She is to be called Mary, in honor of my aunt, who is a pillar of strength to us all, despite her years.'

Such heroism as the ladies practiced deserved more renown than a passing mention in a forgotten diary. What age was this Aunt Mary? Who was she? No last name was given. On the next page poor Dame Sydwell had lost both sons. 'Charlie, who now calls himself Walter, for he will not wear the king's name, was only sixteen. We heard that Knagg was determined his half brother should not be buried in Cromwell's uniform and ripped off his jerkin and helmet, exchanging them for the Cavalier's outfit. I doubt it is true.' The yellow jerkin and the helmet had been under dispute between them through the centuries ever since! 'Knagg died a hero's death? defending Papa.'

Charity lowered the book and dabbed at her moist eyes. 'Papa, you will want to look at

153

this,' she said, and handed him the little diary.

Wainwright snatched it eagerly from her fingers. Strangely, he did not begin at the beginning, but turned toward the back of the book—almost as if he knew where the significant passage was located. Had he read it before? Before he came up with the ghosts' names and relationship? The diary had been sitting enticingly at the top of the trunk, attracting her by those blue ribbons that often indicated a lady's diary. Papa knew she liked to read the ladies' writings. Was papa a fraud?

Yet he had stated categorically there was no ghost in Lady Merton's room, and of course there was not. If he were a mere charlatan, self interest would suggest he would invent one, to please his patroness.

'Most interesting!' he exclaimed, his wicked black eyebrows rising, to give him the look of a satyr. 'I shall show this to Lady Merton. I must have a copy of it, Charity. Merton will not want it to leave the premises. I have ample witnesses that I had identified the ghosts before this confirmation was discovered. If I finish up here soon, I shall be able to have an article ready for the Society's quarterly magazine by June. Unfortunately not in time for the June issue—that is already being printed—but certainly for the September one.

'Now if I could identify the singing nun, I would certainly be elected president of the Society come January—provided Houseman does not get invited to Longleat in the meanwhile. I wonder if Lady Merton would care to write a word to Lady Bath. The Green Lady that haunts the top story of Longleat has been tentatively identified as Lady Louisa Carteret, of course, wife of the second Viscount Weymouth. But the legend does not satisfy me. It is incomplete. If Lady Louisa's lover was murdered, why does his ghost not walk? I daresay I could find it.'

He just glanced at the diary before darting off to Lady Merton. Charity decided he had certainly read it before. Now that he had discovered the story of Knagg, he would get to work on the singing nun, and make equally swift work of it. They would be gone by early next week—interrupting another romance before she could bring it to a successful conclusion. It was always the same, but this time she felt it more deeply, not only in her head, but in her heart. Her heart felt heavy to think of leaving Keefer Hall, and John. Surely he cared for her, at least a little. There must be something she could do.

She went to the window, vaguely wondering if there was any way she could prolong this visit. She noticed St John coming along the path from the woods. Perhaps he had been visiting the hermit, old Ned. The two holy men probably met from time to time. Yet it was odd that St John was behaving in a stealthy manner, peering about to see if anyone was watching, before darting to the stable for his rig.

She soon forgot the minor incident. The diary she had to copy was not large; if she worked quickly, she would have it finished by dinner time.

CHAPTER THIRTEEN

Lady Merton took only a minimal interest in the history of Knagg and Walter.

'How interesting, Mr Wainwright. Yes, of course your daughter may copy the diary, but do tell her to be careful. I can see the paper is fragile.' She had barely glanced at the pertinent pages confirming Wainwright's hypothesis about the relationship between the half brothers.

She was busy having her material comforts removed to the Arras Room, a gloomy chamber hung with ancient Flemish tapestries, chosen for her by Merton because of its hermetical qualities. It had only one window and that was inaccessible by man. The lock on its door did not open with the big brass key that opened most of the other bedroom doors. Best of all, it was directly across the hall from Merton's room. If any pranks were attempted, he would soon discover the perpetrator.

'Very kind of you, milady,' Wainwright said.

'I shall ask my daughter to set about making the copy at once.'

Upon hearing this, Merton saw his hope of Charity's company fly out the window. He made a thorough search of the Arras Room, going through every drawer and cupboard to ensure that Miss Monteith had not sneaked a drugged pigeon in while his back was turned, to awaken from its chemically induced sleep in the middle of the night and fly about the room. After the room was searched, he locked the door and put the only existing key in his own pocket. He would give it to his mama when she retired, and he would stand outside her door until he heard the key turn in the lock. Miss Monteith was to spend the night in her own room in the east wing.

She bore this, as she bore all of Merton's insults, with modest acquiescence, but with spite gleaming in her faded blue eyes.

This done, Merton hobbled down to his study and spent the afternoon frowning over his account ledgers. He was still not entirely happy with that five thousand pounds leaving the family. At the very least, it ought to be used for some good cause that would bear his mama's name. The Lady Merton Scholarship Fund had a fine ring to it, and was certainly useful. He would mention establishing such a fund to St John.

And perhaps he should just take a look at those papers he had signed when he was made treasurer of the St Alban's Trust Fund. If St John alone was, in fact, allowed to sign a check of any denomination, it could be dangerous. Not that St John himself would try anything—he was family after all—but the next incumbent might be less trustworthy. Merton searched through his documents but could not find a copy of the agreement. Demmed odd. He was sure St John had given him a copy. No matter. He would have a look at St John's the next time he was at the vicarage. It was not urgent. St John had a good many years in him yet.

Charity took pains with her toilette for dinner. She felt her pomona-green gown was a trifle too décolleté for a simple country evening at home, but her shawl would modify its dashing style. She looked around for her paisley shawl but could not find it. Surely she had brought it back upstairs last night? She had not worn it today. If it was not downstairs, then a servant must have stolen it. This was always a troublesome situation. She disliked to report it, yet for the hostess to go on harboring a thieving servant was worse. She would wear her white shawl and just casually mention to Lady Merton that she had misplaced her paisley one. If it failed to turn up, Lady Merton would deal with it.

Merton made the effort to be not only civil but ingratiating to his guests at dinner, to make up for the awful luncheon. He enthused over the little diary that confirmed Wainwright's intuitions. Like Charity, he thought, but did not say, that the fellow had read the book before announcing that Knagg and Walter were half brothers.

'Amazing!' he declared. 'You have certainly acquired the knack for ghost hunting, Mr Wainwright. I shall be sure to recommend you to anyone who is being troubled.'

'You would know the Marquess of Bath, I fancy?' Wainwright asked eagerly.

'Certainly I do. I daresay you have been to Longleat, to have a look at the Green Lady?'

'That I have not, but I am highly desirous of going. You might mention my visit here when next you write to Lord Bath.'

'We do not actually correspond. No doubt I shall meet him in the House come autumn. I shall be sure to mention your work here.'

Wainwright frowned. 'Perhaps a line before that time would not go amiss. I am at liberty next week, for no doubt the mystery of the singing nun will be cleared up by then. Tell him I shall be available late next week. Say Thursday, for I must write up an extract on our doings here at Keefer Hall while it is fresh in my mind.'

'What about the mystery of *my* haunting?' Lady Merton asked.

Wainwright just shook his head. He could not like to offend the lady by informing her once again that she had no ghost, only a lively

159

imagination.

The ladies retired to the Blue Saloon after dinner. Charity expected that Lady Merton would leave when the gentlemen arrived, but she sat on. Perhaps she did not look forward to retiring to the Arras Room, where gloomy scenes of battle, worked in thread, awaited her.

'Would you care for a hand of whist, Mr Wainwright?' she suggested. 'We can set up one table and still leave Lewis to entertain your daughter.'

'I would enjoy it very much,' he replied at once.

Merton noticed that he was to provide one of the four bodies at the table. Miss Monteith and his mama would play, of course. They were both demons for cards. He shot one quick, questioning glance at Charity, who carefully concealed her disappointment behind a bland smile.

'I do not feel like cards this evening, Mama,' Merton said. 'This ankle...'

'Why, it will not hurt your ankle to sit at the card table. We shall get a footstool for it. Lewis, speak to Bagot.'

Merton made one more attempt to escape. 'Perhaps Lewis would like to play this evening.'

Lewis soon disabused him of that idea. 'I hate whist. Now if you would like to set up a faro table!'

'Get the cards, dear, and speak to Bagot

about the footstool for John,' Lady Merton said to her younger son.

It seemed rude to continue arguing when Wainwright had expressed approval of a game. Merton wanted Wainwright's good opinion for a certain scheme he was hatching.

Miss Monteith oversaw the placement of chairs at the card table. 'Move the table a little closer to the grate, Bagot. Her ladyship will want the heat at her back. I shall get her favorite pillow.'

When the necessary arrangements had been made, Merton went to the card table while Lewis moved to the sofa to entertain Charity. When Lewis expressed an interest in his ancestor's diary, Charity brought him her copy to read, to protect the fragile original. They were soon discussing it, their heads together over the pages, while Merton played a very inferior hand of whist.

It was Lady Merton who discovered the ghostly apparition hovering at the window. She glanced up from her cards, wordlessly pointed to the window, and turned a ghastly shade of gray just before she fainted dead away. In the ensuing excitement Miss Monteith urged in vain for the gentlemen's assistance in getting Lady Merton to a sofa. They had all darted to the window for a closer look at the ghost, even Merton, who did not wait to retrieve his walking stick but hopped on one foot, leaving Charity to run to her hostess's aid.

She could not resist one quick glance out the window, where she saw what had caused the lady's swoon. A woman, wearing a light gown and cradling an infant in her arms, hovered a moment, then just disappeared in some magical manner.

'Help us! Oh, Lord Merton, do come and give me a hand with her ladyship!' Miss Monteith called.

Merton turned impatiently toward the card table. He saw his mama was recovering. Charity and Miss Monteith were attending her. 'Lewis, give the ladies a hand,' he said. 'I am going after that ... ghost. Toss me my walking stick.'

'I shall go with you, milord,' Wainwright said at once. This was an activity much to his liking. He wished he had his satin-lined cape at hand but could not like to let Merton get a step ahead of him. They went out together, Merton hobbling at a good speed with the help of his thorn walking stick.

Lewis said, 'Mama is all right, is she not? Of course she is. Get the hartshorn, Miss Monteith, and a feather.' His duty done, he pelted off after the others.

Miss Monteith produced a bottle of hartshorn from her pocket while Charity poured Lady Merton a glass of wine. 'It was Meg! I know it was Meg,' Lady Merton moaned. 'This is what comes of John making

162

me leave my own room.'

'I am sure he meant it for the best,' Miss Monteith said with a sharp look at Charity. Make what you can of that, miss! her look said.

'Call Bagot. I must get to bed at once,' Lady Merton whispered.

'Lord Merton has the key in his pocket,' Miss Monteith announced triumphantly.

'My own room, Miss Monteith. I must lie down. I feel shaken to the bone. Miss Wainwright, you will make my excuses to your papa. I am sorry to leave you so much to your own devices, but really...'

'I quite understand, ma'am. I shall call Bagot.'

Charity went into the hallway, where Bagot stood at the open door looking into the distance. 'They have gone chasing the ghost,' he said. 'I hope his lordship is careful of that ankle.'

'Lady Merton needs you,' Charity told him, and darted out into the blackness.

She met her father returning from the chase. 'I could not keep up with those young bucks,' he confessed. 'Even Merton, with his game ankle, got ahead of me. They have gone haring off, but they will not find anything. It is well nigh impossible to pick up the trace in the open air, and with a fairly stiff breeze blowing, too, to dissipate the ether. We shall go back indoors, Charity. How is poor Lady Merton?'

'She has retired, Papa. She asked me to make

163

her apologies.'

'Not necessary. I understand. Let us go in. A glass of wine would not go amiss. I shall take it to the library, to jot down an account of this latest apparition.'

'I—I shall just wait out here a moment, Papa, until the gentlemen return.'

'Suit yourself, but do not stray from the house.'

He left the front door open to give Charity a bit of light. She immediately ran off after Merton and Lewis. Within two minutes they appeared around the side of the house. She could hear their raised voices before she saw them.

'Do be sensible, John,' Lewis said. 'Of course it was not Charity.'

Charity stopped and listened, wondering how she had become involved in the business.

'She was wearing this shawl yesterday,' Merton said grimly. 'She is helping Wainwright, for what purpose one can easily imagine. They want an invitation to Longleat. I have not the least doubt they both read that diary before Wainwright announced the relationship between Knagg and Walter.'

Charity's breast rose and fell angrily. So that was what he thought of her!

'I think the ghost was Meg,' Lewis said firmly.

'Don't be an ass. It was no ghost. We heard the footfalls hitting the ground as we chased

164

after her. If it were not for this demmed busted ankle I would have caught her. Whoever heard of a ghost carrying a lantern?'

'I did not see any lantern,' Lewis objected.

'What else could account for that shaft of light shining on the baby in the woman's arms? And it suddenly disappeared, as soon as she spotted us at the window. It was a dark lantern. She lowered the door that cuts off the light.'

Merton spotted Charity and limped toward her. 'I believe this shawl is yours, ma'am?' he said, handing her her missing paisley shawl.

'Yes, the one that was stolen from my bedroom,' she replied icily. 'Where did you find it?'

'The ghost dropped it. Perhaps you would oblige me by telling me how it came into the hands of the chit who was impersonating Meg this evening?'

'I have not the slightest idea. It was missing from my room when I looked for it before dinner.'

'When a guest has items stolen, it is the custom to report it to her hostess to obviate further trouble. Why did you not tell Mama?'

'Because I did not want to upset her further in her delicate condition. I did mention I could not find it. She paid no heed.'

'Well, it has been found now, under extremely suspicious circumstances.'

'Circumstances that have nothing to do with me!'

'Told you Miss Wainwright had nothing to do with it,' Lewis said.

Merton studied her closely.

'Merton! You cannot truly believe I am involved in this horrid business!' she said angrily.

'Of course not,' he said curtly. His anger was at the theft, but he did not trouble to make this clear. 'How is Mama?' he asked, to be done with the vexing matter.

'She has recovered somewhat. Miss Monteith took her up to her room. Her old room, as you have the key to the Arras Room.'

'By God! That is why Monteith arranged this "ghost." She wanted to get Mama back into her old room, to pull more stunts on her. I shall certainly move her to the Arras Room.'

'But why did she take my shawl?' Charity asked. 'Why is she trying to involve *me*?'

'Pretty plain why,' Lewis said. 'It is because Mr Wainwright refuses to find a ghost in Mama's room. Monteith don't want an expert denying the existence of the ghost when she is at such pains to con Mama into thinking Meg is after her. She is trying to discredit you Wainwrights.'

'That is possible,' Merton admitted. He was not too hard to convince that Charity was innocent.

'That is the answer certainly,' Charity said. 'Your mama is quite convinced it was Meg.'

'I wonder who it was.' He turned to his

brother. 'Lewis, you did not arrange this caper with the Dawson chit?'

'On my honor, I did not. But you are certain about that lantern, Lewis?'

'I am demmed certain it was not a ghost. What else could it have been?'

'Well, if it was not a ghost, the girl ran into the woods,' Lewis said. 'There is no hope of finding her. She was a blonde, definitely. I could see her hair flowing out when the mantle fell down. Where could she be running to? There is nothing in the woods but Old Ned's grotto.'

Charity felt a tingling along the back of her neck. 'How old is Old Ned?' she asked.

'Eh?' Lewis asked, frowning at this irrelevancy. 'He is ancient. Why do you ask?'

'He is not ancient. He is fiftyish,' Merton said with a speculative look at Charity. 'And a spry fiftyish at that. I have seen him darting through the woods like a hare.'

'His white hair is long,' Charity said. 'It would look blond by moonlight. And he is a small man. In that flowing gown he would look like a woman.'

Lewis gave a snort of derisive laughter. 'Next you will be saying he has a child sequestered in his shack.'

'No one actually saw the baby,' Merton said. 'What we saw was a person of indeterminate sex holding a blanket—or Charity's shawl. Imagination did the rest. I believe I shall call on

167

Old Ned.'

'But why would he involve himself in this sort of carry-on?' Charity asked.

'He is mixed up in it somehow,' Lewis said vaguely. 'He was Meg's fellow, remember, before Papa lured her away from him. P'raps he bears us a grudge.'

'We shall soon know,' Merton said. 'We are going to his grotto, Lewis, as soon as we have seen Charity safely into the house. I see Bagot has left the door wide open,' he added with an annoyed *tsk* as they drew nearer.

'That was my fault,' Charity said. 'Papa left it open to give me a little light.'

Merton suddenly realized that Charity had been out alone in the darkness and was diverted from the open door to a reminder that this was unwise of her.

'I did not go far,' she assured him. 'And with both you and Lewis for protection, I feel there would be no harm in my accompanying you to Old Ned's house.'

'Definitely not!' Merton said, and took her elbow to lead her to the open door.

CHAPTER FOURTEEN

'What can happen to Miss Wainwright when you and I are here to protect her?' Lewis demanded. 'You are becoming as bad as Papa,

168

John, never wanting anyone to do anything.'

'What is there to be frightened of?' Charity said, adding her plea to Lewis's.

Merton was soon talked around, for he did not want to appear stuffy in front of her. It was frightening enough, walking through the black forest with only small fragments of sky visible between the towering oaks. Leaves whispered ominous secrets to the wind. Night creatures stirred, disturbed by the incursion of human beings into their private domain. Charity began by offering her arm to Merton to aid his halting walk but ended up clutching his sleeve for protection from the encroaching shadows.

Lewis led the way. 'Old Ned's place is just around the bend,' he whispered. 'I can hear the stream gurgling. We shall creep up on him.'

A lighter-colored square set against the dark hillside told them they had reached Ned's domain. It was in perfect darkness: not a window lit, not a puff of smoke from the chimney. They crept up quietly.

'He is in bed,' Lewis said. 'So much for his burning the midnight oil. I daresay you are right, Charity. He does drink more than he ought.'

'Knock on the door,' Merton said. Lewis tapped lightly.

'He'll not hear that if he is sleeping,' Merton said, and banged loudly with his walking stick. When there was still no reply, he lifted the stick and unceremoniously broke a window. The crash of breaking glass shattered the eerie forest silence.

'Merton!' Charity exclaimed. 'Surely that was not necessary.'

'How else are we to get in? Lewis, kick out the rest of that glass and climb in the window. Open the front door for us.'

'Seems a bit ... I mean to say ... Not quite the thing. A man's house is his castle and all that.'

'This was still my house, the last I heard.'

Lewis picked up a rock to clear away the shards of glass before climbing in. They heard his uncertain call through the window. 'Ned? I say, Ned. Are you home?' Next his head appeared through the gaping window frame. 'He don't seem to be home. I shall open the door.'

Soon the door opened. 'Let us find a lamp,' Merton said, and began feeling around the dark chamber.

'Here, I've got one,' Lewis called from the other side of the room. 'Now if I can find a tinderbox. Ah, here we are.'

He worked the flint, lit the lamp, and a chamber of baroque splendor sprang to life before their eyes. The windows, which appeared to be hung in simple cotton from the outside, revealed brocade drapes within, their grandeur hidden from prying eyes by a cotton lining that faced out. Elegant furnishings were ranged around the room. A striped satin sofa was placed beneath the window, with a bottle of Merton's best claret and a glass on the sofa table before it. An opened magazine lay beside the glass. There was a Persian carpet on the floor, lamps on the tabletops, paintings on the walls. The paintings teased Merton's memory.

'That Canaletto is from our gold guest suite!' he exclaimed.

Lewis picked up a Wedgwood vase. 'This used to be in my room. Mama told me the servants had broken it!'

Merton limped across the room to the other chamber, drawing Charity by the arm with him. The bedchamber was also done up in the first style of elegance, with a canopied bed, more brocade curtains, a desk and toilet table, and all the appurtenances of a gentleman's bedchamber.

'He has got Papa's silver brush set! Really, this is the outside of enough!' Lewis exclaimed. 'I am taking these home with me.' So saying, he gathered up the two brushes and matching comb and shoved them into his pockets.

'I fail to see how this could have been arranged without Mama's contrivance,' Merton said. His eyes moved to the corner of the room, where a case of his best claret stood. There was an empty bottle on the bedside table. His lips tightened in an angry line. 'Bagot has had a hand in this. Other than myself, he is the only one with a key to my wine cellar.'

'If this is how a hermit lives, I shall take up the role myself,' Lewis said. 'Not a sign of a hair shirt or a prie-dieu or a crucifix or any holy pictures. The fellow lives in the lap of luxury, having his meals sent down by Cook. I wonder who does his cleaning up.'

'No one, from the looks of it,' Charity replied.

Her sharp eyes had noticed the dusty surfaces and unswept carpet.

Lewis picked up a tome that lay on the dresser. 'And no holy books either, by Jove, not even a Bible. The old fraud. He is reading Shakespeare. Fancy Old Ned liking Shakespeare.'

'I told you he quoted Shakespeare at us,' Charity reminded him.

'The question is,' Merton said, 'where the deuce is he, in the middle of the night?'

Charity said, 'If he was acting the role of Meg, then perhaps he has gone to report to whomever put him up to it. He is obviously not in this alone.'

'Miss Monteith!' Lewis growled.

Charity frowned. 'Do you remember, when the card table was being set up, Miss Monteith arranged your mama's chair? She said she would want the heat at her back, but it also gave her an excellent view of the window where the ghost appeared.'

'Give her credit, Monteith is awake on all suits,' Lewis murmured.

'And I remember something else, too,' Charity continued. 'I noticed St John coming out of the woods today after he left the Hall. Perhaps he is in on it, too, Merton.'

Lewis said, 'St John does visit Ned from time to time. I don't see that Monteith needed any help. She and Ned between them arranged it. What a set of fools we are. Ned and Monteith are getting their heads together, plotting more mischief, while we come scrambling here busting windows. He will come back sooner or later. We shall wait him out.'

'I have seen enough. I shall deal with Old Ned tomorrow,' Merton said grimly.

'Let us keep an eye peeled on our way home. We might very well run into him,' Lewis suggested.

They extinguished the lamp and left. As a final act of defiance, Lewis took two bottles of the good claret. 'He may count himself fortunate if he does not get one of these over the head.'

It was impossible for three adults, one of them limping, another weighted down with brushes and bottles, to proceed with much silence. They did not intercept, nor could they discover any trace, of Ned lurking about the Hall. As soon as they were home, Merton went limping upstairs. When he returned below, he said, 'I have seen Mama locked into the Arras Room. Monteith is wearing her usual shifty eye. As she has been sitting with Mama since

173

the alleged ghost appeared, she cannot have been in touch with Old Ned yet.'

'Then we shall stick around until he comes,' Lewis said. He set down the bottles of claret and began unloading the brushes from his pockets.

'She will have to come downstairs to admit him,' Merton said.

Charity added, 'She may just speak to him from her bedchamber window. Someone ought to spy from outside.'

'That is true,' Merton agreed. They both looked at Lewis.

'I see I am to be stuck with the dirty work as usual,' he complained. He went to the table, drew the cork from one of the bottles of claret and said, 'I am off. You won't forget to let me know if he shows up at the front door, John? It will be demned uncomfortable, squatting out in the bushes.'

'Take a blanket,' Charity said.

'No thank you, but I shall take this for a chair.' So saying, he stuck the opened wine bottle in his pocket and took up Merton's footstool. Charity held the door for him, then returned to Merton.

She said, 'We can see the bottom of the staircase from the sofa in the corner. With all the lights out, Miss Monteith will not see us hiding.'

'There is no need for you to miss your sleep,' he said politely, although he liked the notion of sitting in the dark with Charity for an hour or so.

'I could not possibly sleep with all these mysterious goings-on. I shall just wrap myself up in this shawl—which I did *not* give to Ned—and make myself comfortable.'

'You now have two sticks with which to beat me over the head. Once more, I apologize.' Merton drew the cork on the other bottle of claret and they were soon privately ensconced on the sofa. 'Should we not put out the lamps?' Charity said.

'The hall is still lit. Bagot has not locked up yet. Monteith will wait until everyone is asleep. Ah, there is Bagot now. I shall have a word with him. Bagot, if you have a moment, please.' Bagot hastened forward.

'I have just returned from Old Ned's castle, where I found a case of this,' Merton said, pointing to the wine bottle. 'Only you and I have the key to the cellar, Bagot. I most assuredly did not give him the wine. Perhaps you can explain this mystery to me.'

Bagot blinked in confusion. 'Why, we have always supplied the hermit with the necessities of life, milord. Since your late papa's time.'

'I consider this excellent wine one of life's luxuries, not necessities. Surely a hermit, devoted to a life of prayer and self-effacement, can do without a Canaletto painting, and the final straw—Papa's dresser set. Really, this is going a good deal too far.'

'His lordship's orders were to give him whatever he asked for, within reason.'

'It has gone beyond reason!'

Bagot looked uncomfortable. 'I did tell her ladyship you would miss the Canaletto—although you did not miss it for three years.'

Merton ignored Charity's little explosion of laughter. 'Then Mama is aware of all the depredations Ned is making on my estate?' he asked haughtily.

'I would never undertake to supply him so lavishly on my own recognizance, milord!'

'I see. Have you ever seen Ned lurking about the house, perhaps talking to someone?'

'He never leaves the woods. The way we handle it, milord, young Jamie, the footboy, takes down the meals and brings Ned's written orders to me.'

'*Orders!* Who the devil does he think he is?'

'I should have said requests. If the request is for something unusual, I discuss it with her ladyship. A good many books have been leaving the library over the years, for instance. Old Ned is a great reader. Mind you, he always sends the books back after a few weeks.'

Charity listened eagerly. When Bagot had finished, she said, 'Did he actually have the nerve to ask for the late Lord Merton's dresser set?'

'Ah, no, that was a gift from her ladyship. Old Ned did hint for a keepsake. I think, myself, it was his lordship's watch he was after,

but your lordship'—he bowed to Merton—
'had already taken that.'

'And a fine timepiece it is, too.' Merton
grinned, drawing his papa's old Grebuet watch
from his pocket.

'So the upshot is, Old Ned has been living
high on the hog all these years at no expense,
without doing a hand's turn of work,' Charity
said. 'He made a better deal selling Meg than if
he had married her. It hardly seems fair.'

'It ain't,' Merton agreed, 'but in the future
Old Ned's perquisites will be limited to the
same food and wine the servants drink. He may
have what he requires for modest comfort. His
days of living like a lord are over.'

'You mean you are going to let him stay on!'
Charity gasped.

Merton blinked in astonishment. 'It was
Papa's order. He made a bargain with Old
Ned. He kept it, and naturally I, as his heir,
shall do the same. Old Ned has always been
with us, for as long as I can remember.'

'Naturally. That explains it,' she said
resignedly.

'Was there anything else, milord?' Bagot
asked.

'Yes, I think Miss Wainwright would like
some tea and perhaps a sandwich.'

Bagot bowed and left.

'Your mama is very generous, to treat Old
Ned so lavishly,' Charity said. 'It is her guilty
conscience that accounts for it, of course.'

'I should think so. And it is her easy capitulation to all of Old Ned's extravagant requests that has given him the idea she is easy plucking. My only question is why Ned risked such a good thing. Perhaps he just became bored.'

'I daresay Miss Monteith put him up to it. She was not on to such a good thing, was she? You mentioned she was only an upstairs maid before your mama took her on as her companion.'

'That is true, but she is on to a much better thing now. What does she actually gain from all this ghost business? A firmer grip on Mama,' he said doubtfully. 'Perhaps a little something in Mama's will.'

'Surely she is older than Lady Merton? Why should she live longer—unless...' She gazed at Merton while he puzzled out her meaning.

'Good God! Are you suggesting she is trying to get herself written into Mama's will and will then make sure Mama dies before her?'

'It is possible. And Lady Merton spoke to Penley only the other day. Merton, is it possible she changed her will?'

Merton slowly set down his glass, strode from the room and up the staircase, and pounded on his mother's door.

CHAPTER FIFTEEN

'Miss Monteith, is that you?' Lady Merton called through the door.

'It is John. Let me in, Mama.'

Lady Merton rose from her bed, where she had been seeking consolation in a perusal of the Psalms, and unlocked the door. 'No white birds—so far,' she said, trying to smile, but her dark eyes were troubled and her face was pinched with fatigue or fear.

Merton felt a stab of pity, followed by a burning anger against whoever was doing this to his mother. He spoke calmly as he led her back to her bed. 'That is good news,' he said, tucking her in. Then he drew a chair up to her bedside. 'Mama, I must know. Did you change your will the other day at Eastleigh?'

'No, dear. I told you, I discussed giving St John five thousand for his fund. My will does not come into it. You know Lewis gets my entire estate. If the five thousand has been taken out of the estate before I die, then he gets the remainder. Why do you ask?'

'You must not leave Miss Monteith anything. Not a sou, not a hairpin.'

Lady Merton smiled fondly. 'What would be the point, dear? She is five years older than I. Barring any unforeseen ill luck on my part, I should outlive her.'

It was that ill luck on her part that concerned him. 'You will not change your will. Promise!'

Lady Merton's mind was not on murder. She did not leap to the conclusion that someone was trying to kill her, only that Merton feared she meant to give away his brother's inheritance. 'I promise.'

He breathed a sigh of relief 'Now for number two. About Old Ned, Mama. It is folly the way you pamper him.'

'Old Ned prays for me. And you know it was your papa's wish that I look after him.'

'Shall I tell you how he repays your kindness? Yes, I think you deserve to know. It was Old Ned who was masquerading as Meg tonight outside the window, frightening the life out of you.'

'Don't be absurd! Ned never leaves the forest. And why would he do such a thing? He is very happy with his books and leisure to study and pray. Very likely rumors of our hauntings have reached the village and some youngsters were playing a prank on us. The ghost did not look much like Meg, now you mention it. When she comes to my window, she is a more ghostly form, rather loose and weaving, you know.'

More like a stuffed dummy on a stick or rope, Merton interpreted, but he knew there was no point in saying so.

'He does leave the forest,' Merton said. 'He was not at home this evening when I . . . visited

180

him after the so-called ghost disappeared into the woods. I believe it was Ned.'

Lady Merton just smiled indulgently. 'I know you do not believe in ghosts, John. If you had had my experiences, you would not be so certain.'

'Your experiences or your guilty conscience, Mama?' he asked gently.

'Both. Truth to tell, I do feel very guilty about—oh, so many things.'

'You are referring to Meg specifically, I think.'

'It is mostly Meg who bedevils my conscience, of course. That episode was so horrid a part of my life that I try to forget it, but lately it has all been coming back. You have no idea what it was like—a nightmare is nothing to it, and believe me I have had considerable experience of them as well. You know your papa and I were not getting along. I saw him kissing Meg—and she was so very pretty. One of those blond, dimpled lasses, you know. Even with a child on the way, she was still beautiful. I told him, It is Meg or me. Of course he had no choice but to turn her off. She was not due for two months, but with the commotion of my hysterics and her being turned out of the house, she delivered her child that very night—alone in a ditch. You might as well say I killed her and the child—your papa's child, for that is what happened to them both.'

'You are mistaken there, Mama. She was

not alone. She only went to the dower house. The doctor was called. You must not blame yourself for all that.'

'No, no, you have got it all wrong. There was a birth in the dower house around that time, but it was not Meg's child. I told you cousin Algernon and his wife were there. That was not quite true; the lady was not his wife but another lady who had been widowed for a year. Her family sent her to Scotland to hide her shame, but she wanted to have her *accouchement* in England, and Algernon arranged with your papa to bring her here so that his wife would not find out. It was Algernon's friend who had a child at the dower house. I never met the lady. Your papa felt it would not be proper for me to visit her. She gave the child up for adoption and returned to London. The child was St John. Your papa arranged it all very discreetly. The St Johns were a childless couple, getting on in years. Your papa was fond of the lad and paid for his education and so on. I have always kept an eye on him, which is why I asked you to give him the living here.'

'You mean St John is actually a blood relation? Why was I never told this?'

'I try never to think or speak of that period of my life. And St John, who knows, of course, is rather sensitive of his illegitimacy. He feels that for a minister it is better to have been a poor but legitimate orphan than a noble bastard. We set about the story that he was left on our doorstep in a basket.'

Merton sat, deep in thought. 'This occurred around the time you sent Meg off?'

'A while later, dear. About two weeks later, I think. I had no idea, at the time, that Meg was dead. Your papa did not tell me; we never spoke of her again once she left. I eventually heard rumors from the servants, years later. I did not believe them. They always made a Cheltenham tragedy out of trifles. I scarcely listened to them—so selfish. I was *enceinte* myself with you by then, and your papa was happy. Then all these years later when the ghost began to appear, I decided I must take myself by the scruff of the neck and atone for my past sins. I asked Miss Monteith if it was true, about Meg and the chid dying. She confirmed it—reluctantly. She does not blame me in the least, dear. You are quite mistaken to think she holds any grudge.'

Merton listened to this with a doubting ear. Those ghostly apparitions did not suggest innocence on Monteith's part.

'I do not know what I should have done without her these few months,' his mama continued. 'She and St John have been my strength, John, for I do not like to trouble you with my problems. You have enough in your dish. Five thousand is a small price to pay for peace of mind. Not that money can buy forgiveness, but as St John says, charity covers a multitude of sins. Perhaps the St Alban's fund will save the lives of a mother and a child, to atone for Meg and her infant. That is my little consolation.'

'I daresay St John will use the money wisely.'

'He is a wonderful man. Such a consolation to me. If there is nothing else, dear, I think I can sleep now. Talking about it helps.'

'I shall lock the door when I leave.'

She gave him an indulgent smile, as if humoring a lunatic, but she listened closely to hear the door lock behind him. When he returned below, Merton was disappointed to see Wainwright sitting with his daughter.

'I have been telling Papa all about the strange goings-on here, Merton,' she said. 'I hope you do not mind? Papa is the soul of discretion. What had Lady Merton to say?'

'She has not changed her will and has promised not to do so,' he said.

Wainwright sipped his excellent claret and prepared to pontificate on the matter. 'This is not my field of expertise,' he admitted. That never stopped him from delivering an opinion, however, and he continued, 'But I feel obliquely involved as your pranksters are employing sham ghosts. Such things give ghosts a bad name.'

'Just so,' Merton agreed politely.

'Tell him what you said, Papa,' Charity urged.

'Not that it is my concern—nor yours either, young lady. I do not approve of your capering about dark forests at night visiting hermits. However, as Lord Merton wants my opinion, it is as follows. Number one, you have this hermit fellow with the world at his fingertips. Why should he rock the boat? The Monteith woman has got herself a pretty soft berth as well. The only one who stands to get any money out of the scheme is St John. I refer, of course, to the money in the St Alban's fund. A scheme of this sort is bound to have money at the root. What do you know of him? He would not be the first scoundrel to hide behind the cloth.'

'He is my cousin,' Merton said, and explained with a blush his cousin Algernon's part in the matter.

Wainwright did him the courtesy of listening without interruption. The excellence of the claret made it an agreeable pastime. When Merton had finished, Wainwright resumed the center of the stage, his favorite spot.

'So what you have is two births at about the same time. Lady Merton heard nothing of Meg or her infant dying at the time. Who is to say they did die?'

'There is a grave in the graveyard bearing the proper names and date,' Merton pointed out.

'Ah, just so. The grave. But there seems to be some suspicion that the grave does not contain the body of the child. Perhaps the child did not die. What I am getting at is that your late papa came up with this ruse of his cousin's lady

185

friend at the dower house to keep from his good wife that he had Meg installed there. He wanted a son—if he could not have a legitimate one—well, he could have t'other sort at least. Better than nothing. You mentioned a two-week lapse between Meg's departure from Keefer Hall and your cousin's arrival at the dower house with the *enceinte* lady in tow. It is possible Meg was kept there during that time awaiting the birth. When Meg delivered and died, your papa set about the story that the baby had died as well—both of them buried together. He had these St Johns adopt his son. St John, the vicar, discovered it somehow and decided to cut himself in on the family fortune.'

Merton disliked to admit that the man could be right, but as he thought over that dim and murky past, he thought it was possible. There was that strange rumor about Meg being alone in her grave.

'How could St John have discovered all this?' he asked. 'Mama says he believes he is cousin Algernon's by-blow.'

'Who else but Meg's sister could have told him?' Wainwright asked. 'You may be sure she knows the ins and outs of it. I would not be surprised if she was sent to the dower house to keep her sister company during her confinement. Mind you, she is not likely to admit it.'

'Bagot would know,' Merton said, and went into the hallway to speak to the butler.

186

He wore an eager look when he returned. 'You were quite right, Mr Wainwright. Miss Monteith did accompany her sister. Bagot says Algernon and his lady friend were at the dower house at the same time that Meg was there. Miss Monteith assisted at the lady's confinement. An even stranger twist has been added to the story. The midwife set about the tale that the lady had been wearing a mask during her confinement. The midwife never got a look at her face. It was supposed at the time that this was to conceal the lady's identify, but it is hardly likely the midwife would have recognized some dashing London lady.'

'Aha!' Wainwright exclaimed. 'But she would have recognized Meg Montieth fast enough.'

Charity sat, struck momentarily silent by the bizarre and gruesome image of a masked woman giving birth. 'But did Bagot say the masked woman died during childbirth?' she asked.

'No,' Merton said. 'It was described as a very difficult labor. Perhaps Meg died after the midwife had left.'

'So that is how it was worked,' Wainwright said with a sapient look. 'Meg's child was not born the night your mama put her out. She went to the dower house and stayed until her time was due. Your papa hired Algernon and his lady friend for his little charade. That would give him an unexceptionable excuse to

187

visit Meg. It was a pretext to fool Lady Merton. Algernon's widowed lady was not *enceinte* at all. Meg died after the midwife left, but the much-wanted boy child survived and was kept under wraps at the dower house, posing as Algernon's by-blow. Your papa next arranged with a compliant undertaker to say there was a babe in the coffin with this Meg, and the thing was done. The servants would not be slow to come up with this lurid tale about Meg dying in the ditch. They like a touch of melodrama. Someone involved was indiscreet and let out that there was no child buried with Meg. We shall never discover at this late date who did so, but there would have been a few servants involved in the charade.'

'That is a very interesting hypothesis, Mr Wainwright. I shall sleep on it,' Merton said with a new air of respect in his manner.

'It is time for us to hit the feather tick as well, Charity. I shall just run along to the Armaments Room to see that all is quiet there. I will not be long.'

Merton welcomed the moment alone with Charity. 'Your papa has a wise head on his shoulders, when he puts it to some better use than looking for ghosts.'

'Do you think he might be right?'

'There is one way to find out.'

'You mean to confront Miss Monteith?'

'No, I mean to dig up Meg's coffin and see just who—or what—besides herself is buried in it.'

'That will require permission from the authorities, will it not?'

'Indeed it will. I mean to make the thing entirely public. Unfortunately, it is too late to question cousin Algernon; he is dead, and Mama does not have the lady's name. I daresay she was a London actress. Algernon would have been familiar with the profession.'

Charity drew a frowning sigh. 'Your poor mama. It must have been horrid to be married to Lord Merton.'

Merton gave her a worried glance. 'All that was long ago. We have improved since those days. But the ghosts come back to haunt us.'

'It is a good thing you have Papa here to handle them for you. We shall make a believer of you yet, Merton.'

'It is your father's common sense that impresses me more. He wove the strands of the story together with commendable promptness and ingenuity. He might even be right.'

They were interrupted by the sound of footsteps approaching the door. 'All is quiet in the Armaments Room,' Wainwright announced. 'Come along, Charity. We do not want to keep Merton up so late.'

Merton looked more frustrated than pleased at the interruption, but he said good night to his guests with a polite face, and they parted.

189

CHAPTER SIXTEEN

Lord Merton met with his colleagues over breakfast the next morning to discuss the fruits of his night's pondering and their strategy for the job ahead. He had already talked it over with Wainwright the evening before when he went to his room to speak of other matters. He assumed Wainwright had told the others. He noticed that Lewis and Charity were sitting with their heads together when he entered the breakfast room. They drew apart hastily, with guilty looks, just before she gave him a heavy frown. She was not happy to be excluded from active participation in the affair.

'You have told them?' he asked Wainwright.

'That I have. They agree it is a fine plan. Hoist by his own petard!' Wainwright laughed. 'Set a ghost to catch a ghost. I will be happy to participate. Smoke, I think, in lieu of steam. You will want a damp fire, to cause the greatest amount of smoke and the least light. The open air will dissipate the smell.'

'I doubt he will be close enough to catch the scent,' Merton said. 'We shall light the fire when we see him come out of the vicarage. With luck it will not be necessary to open Meg's grave, but I shall arrange the formalities, in case it comes to that.'

After breakfast Charity followed Merton to

his office. 'I want to be Meg,' she said.

'It is out of the question. Lewis will be Meg.'

'But he is too big! No one would believe he is a woman.'

'It will be dark, and they will not see him at close range.'

'I can talk Papa around, if that is what concerns you. He will not really mind.'

'I will mind. We don't know what will happen. There might be trouble. This is for me to handle as I see fit,' he said more sternly than he wanted to, but it would be unthinkable to put an innocent young lady at risk. If anything should happen to Charity . . . 'You shall remain at Keefer Hall.'

'Merton! You could not be so mean! At least let me go to the graveyard!' His harsh scowl softened to a reluctant smile. She saw it and knew he was wavering. 'Please! Pretty please.'

'Very well, but you must stay well out of the fray. I would not want anything to happen to you.'

She gave a saucy look. 'This is the first nice thing you have ever said to me, Merton.'

'Indeed!'

'I shall leave now, before you change your mind—and decide to let me be Meg. I don't think I would really enjoy that.'

'You only came here to get yourself included in the outing!'

'Yes, one learns how to manage recalcitrant gentlemen, with practice. Winton suggested

191

the way to achieve my aim was to ask for more than I wanted.'

'I take leave to tell you, you are a managing female, Miss Wainwright.'

'Why, thank you,' she said, dropping a curtsy and darting out the door.

Merton watched her leave. He rubbed his chin thoughtfully. So she was on terms of some intimacy with Lewis. That might be a problem.

At ten Merton rode off to Eastleigh to set in motion the necessary formalities for the exhumation of the mortal remains of Meg Monteith and her infant son, Roger. By noon all the concerned parties were aware of the fact when they gathered in the Blue Saloon. Lady Merton had been informed of the charade and was in the boughs. She immediately sent off to the vicarage for St John, who came scrambling to Keefer Hall to inveigh against the scheme.

'Can you not speak sense to Merton, Mr Wainwright?' he said, choosing this unlikely ally to buttress his objections to the plan. 'God only knows what new ghosts might be unleashed.'

'Hardly new ghosts,' Wainwright said thoughtfully. 'Meg and her son already haunt the house, do they not, despite my being unable to make contact? Perhaps it will lay their ghosts to rest. It will all be done discreetly, Vicar, never fear.'

'Yes, certainly,' Merton said. 'It will take a couple of days to get the exhumation order in place. I shall arrange for men to open the grave tomorrow night after darkness falls, when everyone is in bed. Around midnight.'

'It sounds like jolly good sport. I would not miss it for a monkey,' Lewis said, smiling.

'This is not a public entertainment, Lewis,' his brother chided. 'There will be no one there but the grave diggers, myself, and an impartial witness appointed by the magistrate. I have suggested Mr Wainwright. The magistrate has agreed.'

'Happy to oblige,' Wainwright said with a nod. 'There is no saying; some supernatural occurrence may take place. A disturbed grave is no light matter. Perhaps a vicar would be useful as well,' he suggested, looking at St John.

'I will not show approval of this outrageous scheme by taking any part in it,' St John replied. 'I want it firmly understood that I disapprove. Really, Merton, you might have a little respect for your mama's wishes.'

Merton just smiled a lazy smile. 'Mama wishes for peace from the past. I am endeavoring to accomplish that for her.'

'What will it accomplish, even if the child is not in the grave?' St John demanded. 'It only proves the child is buried elsewhere. I hope you do not plan to dig up the entire graveyard?'

'I disagree,' Merton said. 'The gravestone says the child is buried in Meg's grave. If the child is not there, then it indicates he was not buried. One assumes a corpse was not left above ground. In short, Vicar, I feel it will go some way toward proving that Meg's son did not die.'

'Of course he died!' Miss Monteith exclaimed. 'I was there. I held the poor wee thing in my arms as it gasped its last breath. I found Meg in the meadow, all alone,' she added hastily.

'If it is in the grave,' Merton said blandly, 'then both mother and child will be reburied and that will be the end of it.'

'But what if it is not?' Lady Merton asked.

'Then I shall have to take steps, Mama.' He looked for a moment at the vicar, then turned his dark eyes to Miss Monteith, before continuing to speak to his mother. 'But pray do not concern yourself. And now if you will excuse me, I must go and speak to my workmen, to see which of them will be free tomorrow night. Come along, Lewis.' They rose, bowed and left the room together.

When they were beyond the door, Lewis said, 'I shall get my mount and hide behind the stable to follow St John when he leaves.'

'No, go on foot,' Merton said. 'And if he does not go directly to Old Ned, see where he goes, then return to keep an eye on Ned. I must know if they meet or if a message is sent.'

'Do I stop St John or just watch?'

'Just watch. I do not want their messages intercepted, but only to confirm that they are in touch. And, Lewis, I understand you have been instructing Miss Wainwright how to *manage* me.' He regarded his brother with a fiery eye.

'Really, John. Why should she not come along? You never want her to do anything. You ought to watch that managing streak. You are becoming just like Papa.'

'Papa would have boxed your ears for this impertinence. Run along, wretch.'

Wainwright soon left the saloon as well, taking his daughter with him. 'Lord Merton has allowed me to visit his room this morning, in hopes of speaking to the singing nun,' he explained to the others.

He and Charity did not go above stairs immediately, but nipped smartly into Bagot's little room. Bagot, too, had been pressed into service in the post of watchman. As they suspected, Lady Merton left the saloon alone a moment later and went upstairs. Miss Monteith remained behind to have a word with St John. All was going according to plan.

'Do you think it will work?' Charity asked her father.

'If we are on the right track, it cannot fail. What would *you* do if confronted with this debacle? Get a skeleton of a child into that grave, right?'

'But how? Where will they find one?'

'It will be difficult but not impossible. There must be infants buried nearby.'

Bagot cleared his throat and said, 'Or

perhaps they will use animal bones. There are dozens of dogs buried on the estate. In the darkness of night all that would be seen is a parcel of bones swaddled in some decaying cloth. No one will be eager to handle the remains.'

'It sounds horrid!' Charity exclaimed.

'Aye,' her father said, 'but not so horrid as what is being done to that poor lady. I knew all along there was no ghost in her room; this will prove it. My reputation is at stake. I shall write up a monograph for the Society, to make them aware of such stunts in the future.'

Charity said, 'I shall go abovestairs and begin to make up the wig. I fear I must sacrifice my round bonnet to the cause. I shall need something headshaped to attach the wool to. Merton said you would provide me with the yellow wool, Bagot?'

He handed her a ball of wool, artfully concealed in a teapot. 'You might find a doll in the nursery to use for the child,' he added.

'Be sure you lock your door, Charity,' Wainwright cautioned. 'We do not want Miss Monteith sniffing out our little secret. She must be on needles this morning, poor woman. Let it be a lesson to her. And now I believe I shall go to visit the singing nun.' Charity gave him a sharp look. 'I do have Merton's permission, my dear. He was very civil about it.'

They went upstairs together, still discussing their scheme. As expected, Mr Wainwright did not utter any serious objections to Charity's participating.

'If Merton thinks it is safe, then you may come along,' he said with very little interest.

Miss Monteith's presence at lunch made any private discussion impossible, but after lunch the Wainwrights and the Dechastelaine brothers used a tour of the gardens as an excuse for more planning.

They went out into the spring sunshine to stroll along the paths and down the steps of the parterre. An allée guarded by a double row of poplars led to a fountain as the focal point of the allée.

'St John did not go directly to visit Old Ned, John,' Lewis said. 'He drove off toward home in his gig, but he came back on foot later. They were closeted together for the better part of an hour.'

Merton said, 'I spotted St John making a tour of the graveyard—no doubt looking for an infant grave he could plunder. I doubt he will sink to that. It would be too noticeable.'

Wainwright listened, then spoke. 'What do you suppose they will do after you have exposed them, Merton?'

'St John will have to change careers. He is certainly unfit to be a man of the cloth. With his education he will soon find work elsewhere—teaching perhaps. It will be for Mama to decide Miss Monteith's fate, but I will not have her under my roof.'

'I am happy to hear it. You might recall I fingered her as a malign influence the first time I met her.'

'So you did.' Merton nodded. He thought Wainwright could be a clever man if he would only let up on this hobbyhorse of his.

'And Old Ned?' Lewis asked. 'The place will not seem the same without our hermit.'

'Perhaps he will become a true hermit,' Merton said. 'We must wait and see how deeply he is involved in all of this. At the very least, my paintings will be returned and my wine cellar locked. My best claret!'

Charity *tsked*. 'I think that bothers you more than the rest, Merton.'

'No, what they have done to Mama bothers me more.'

The terraced gardens, shining under the spring sun, seemed an unlikely place to be discussing the heinous goings-on at Keefer Hall. It was soon clear that Mr Wainwright felt the call of his profession. He turned to look back at the cloisters.

'Did you hear that?' he asked, cupping his ear.

'I heard nothing,' Merton replied. Neither had Charity or Lewis.

'Surely you heard the mournful singing? It came from the cloisters. The singing nun! I must investigate.'

'I shall go with you,' Lewis said at once, and they hurried off together.

198

Merton offered Charity his arm. 'Alone at last,' he said with a smile. They reached the allée and began walking toward the fountain.

'It was kind of you to let Papa investigate your bedchamber,' she said.

'If it is haunted, then it is best to remove the ghosts before ... before he leaves.'

'We shall be leaving soon. Once Lady Merton is satisfied that she has no ghost in her chamber, there will be no reason to remain.'

'Why, you are forgetting the singing nun, ma'am.'

'You do not believe in that. That is not why we were invited.'

'Have you forgotten I promised you a party?'

'It will be some time before you are able to dance, with that lame ankle,' she pointed out.

'True, you may have to remain a few weeks.'

'We seldom stay anywhere as long as that,' she said wistfully.

'I fancy your papa will stay awhile at least when I tell him what I have in mind.'

Charity felt a rush of blood to her head. 'What—whatever do you mean, Merton?' she asked in a choked voice.

'I have sent a footman off to Lord Bath at Longleat, as your father mentioned an interest in visiting it. I extolled your papa's powers and mentioned that he is in the neighborhood. Longleat is not so far from Keefer Hall. It seems a shame not to continue on to Wiltshire, while he is already halfway there.'

Her heart settled down to a dull, disappointed thud. 'That was very kind of you. He will be *aux anges* to visit Lord Bath.'

'You, I think, do not share your father's enthusiasm for this peripatetic life-style, Charity.'

'To tell the truth, I have become a little tired of it. It seems I no sooner get home than we are off again.'

'Perhaps it is time for you to settle down,' he said, watching for her reaction.

She just shook her head. 'Tell that to Papa. While there is a haunted house in England, he will not settle down.'

'I shall speak to him,' was all he said.

'Oh, no! You must not. This is his whole life. He would sink into a slough of despond if he were deprived of his ghost hunting.'

'There is no reason *he* must stop, if it amuses him.'

Charity did not think her life would be very amusing at home alone with only the housekeeper and servants for company. She had never had time to make a close circle of friends. Their friends were really the members of the Society and their families. It seemed that she had once more lost out on a potential *parti* due to her father's work. They would be off to Longleat to work with the Green Lady, and Lord Merton would eventually find himself a bride from among his own set.

She watched as the water splashed from the fountain. The individual droplets caught the sun and glowed prismatically as they fell into the basin below.

'They did not have such a lovely fountain at Radley Hall,' she said sadly. She sat on the edge of the basin and dabbled her fingers in the water, wishing she could stay on here for months—forever, with Merton.

CHAPTER SEVENTEEN

Dinner was a somber meal, with Lady Merton looking daggers at her son. She showed not the least interest in Mr Wainwright's announcement that he had solved the mystery of the singing nun's visits to Lord Merton's bedchamber, which had been a monk's cell when the nun was alive.

'It was a love affair,' Wainwright announced. 'She used to slip into her young man's room via a rope ladder he let down from his window for her in the dead of night. I fear the lady was what we would describe as "no better than she should be." Her family sent her to a nunnery for her frowardness. She espied Brother Francis—that was her lover's name—when he was working in the priory's knot garden. By those little ruses a cunning lady can always contrive, she arranged to meet him at

201

night, after the other nuns and brothers had retired. As autumn cooled to winter, the meetings moved to Brother Francis's cell.

'The prioress happened to check on the nun's bed one night and found it empty. She notified the clergyman in charge of the priory, who called the nun's father. It was a local family. The father watched his daughter's movements the next night from the shadows. He followed her to her lover's cell. He drew his sword and made a lunge at Brother Francis. The nun leaped forward to protect him, thinking her father would not harm her. Too late; the steel found its mark. It was the nun who was killed. Hence the bloodstain on the ghost's bodice. Brother Francis was given a harsh penalty. The story was hushed up to protect the girl's father from a charge of murder.'

Wainwright had spent some time working his findings up into a dramatic presentation. He was disappointed with its lukewarm reception.

'Is that so?' Lady Merton asked in a distracted way, and immediately went on to inquire if he would like some more ragout.

It was only Lewis who listened with any genuine eagerness. 'Who was she?' he asked.

'The nun's name was Philomela. I did not get a family name. Philomela, of course, is a poetic name for the nightingale. "And Philomele her song with teares doth steepe." Spenser, I

202

believe. Your unfortunate Philomela had some small fame in the priory for her charming voice. She has been steeping the cloister with her tearful tune all these years.'

'I wonder the chamber ain't awash. What does she want?' Lewis asked.

Wainwright gave an indulgent smile. 'Ghosts' tears are dry. They have no physical substance. What Philomela wishes is only the privilege of remaining here, waiting for Brother Francis's return.'

'She will have a long wait.' Lewis laughed.

'I'm sure no one is trying to stop her,' Lady Merton said.

Wainwright continued, not entirely happy with these intrusions into his soliloquy. 'By day she walks the cloisters, singing, and by night she goes to Lord Merton's room, which is still Brother Francis's cell to her. It is not uncommon for ghosts to ignore renovations to the spot they haunt. She is by no means a malign ghost. Her spirit is fading. Another hundred years and I fancy you will be rid of her. Of course I darted to the library to look for confirmation of her tale as soon as she imparted it to me, but alas! I have found no proof.'

Merton was impressed with Wainwright's inventiveness, if not his ghost-hunting ability or his veracity. 'Very interesting,' he said. 'And Philomela was active this afternoon, was she? I wonder what accounts for it.'

'Why, it would be the full moon,' Wainwright explained. 'Ghosts are activated by the full moon. Of course midnight is their favored hour. At midnight tonight I fancy we will have all your ghosts up and about.'

Miss Monteith opened her lips to speak—an entirely new thing for her at the table. 'The word *loony* comes from the French for moon, *la lune*,' she said, smiling spitefully at Wainwright. Her intention was to imply that Wainwright was loony, but she was not much of a hand at satire.

He smiled tolerantly and went into a long dissertation on the effects of the full moon on the spirit world.

The ladies retired to the Blue Saloon after dinner. As Charity expected, her hostess and Miss Monteith left shortly after the gentlemen joined them. Lady Merton, putting her fingers to her head, mentioned a megrim.

'I shall get you a small draft of laudanum,' Miss Monteith said.

As soon as they had left, Merton said, 'That laudanum will ensure that Mama sleeps well—and does not call for her companion over the next few hours. Monteith, I fancy, will not be at Mama's disposal.'

'When do we go?' Lewis asked eagerly.

'Not for several hours yet. Shall we have a game of whist to pass the time? Monteith will be lurking about to keep an eye on us. We shall ostensibly retire at eleven.'

They played a few desultory hands of whist. No one's mind was really on the game. Bagot slipped in to inform them, at ten-thirty, that Miss Monteith had just gone to the kitchen for a cup of cocoa. She had asked, en route, what the others were doing.

At eleven they abandoned the game and all but Lewis made a rather noisy retreat to their bedrooms. Within five minutes Lewis came scraping at Merton's door to inform him that Monteith had just sneaked out by the kitchen door and was headed to the vicarage.

'Any sign of Ned?' Merton asked.

'No, very likely he went along earlier. I have got the outfit ready. Shall we go?'

'Give a light tap on Wainwright's and Charity's doors.'

The four conspirators met in the Blue Saloon, which was unlit but for a ray of lamplight from the hall. They were all dressed in dark clothing.

'We shall slip out by the library door in case they are having the house watched,' Merton said. 'The yews around the little garden there will conceal the opening of the door.'

They did as he suggested. The full moon shone palely in a misty sky. Charity's first impression was of a pearly fairyland, with fog beginning to form close to the ground, but as her eyes became accustomed to the darkness, she noticed that her vision was not seriously impeded. Merton rooted in the yew hedge for the sack containing damp wood and a flint box that Bagot had concealed there. Charity and Lewis also retrieved a bundle. They looked all about, and when they were assured that no one was watching, they stealthily made their way toward the graveyard, darting along in the shadows of tall, whispering trees.

Charity used Merton's limp as an excuse to lend him her arm, but in fact he was hardly limping at all now. She felt he could dance sooner than the two weeks he had mentioned. Was the limp recovering so slowly as an excuse to keep her at Keefer Hall for the promised rout party? When his hand slid down her arm to seize her fingers, she knew he had forgotten all about his limp. He looked up at the diffused moonlight and said, 'This seems too fine a night to waste on ghost hunting.'

'You do not want to let Papa hear you say that,' she said, smiling. 'There is nothing better than ghost hunting in his world.'

He just looked at her, with the shadows flickering over his face and hiding his eyes. 'His world is not necessarily our world, Charity.' His fingers tightened, but he said no more.

They soon reached the graveyard. By moonlight it was an eerie sight. Ghostly white monuments stood guard over the bodies of long-dead relatives. A spreading elm just beyond the burial ground stood out in stark silhouette against the silver sky. In such a place it was easy to believe in ghosts. In the distance a

206

dog howled at the moon, causing a collective shiver to scuttle up their spines. The fence of dark yews provided concealment for Lewis's transformation into the ghost of Meg Monteith.

'Have you got the doll?' he asked Charity.

She handed him her bundle: an ancient doll from the nursery, swaddled in a linen serviette.

'This demmed wool wig don't flow like real hair,' he complained.

'Never mind. Just tie the bonnet under your chin so it does not fly off at the wrong moment. They will not get more than a glimpse of you from afar.'

'I don't know how you ladies get about in these skirts. I shall fall flat on my face if they come chasing after me.'

Merton listened as he set up the damp wood near Meg's grave, the fire to be concealed by a large block of wood placed in front of it. He silently watched the vicarage. At eleven-thirty the door opened and three figures skulked out.

'Who is the third? That ain't Ned,' Lewis whispered.

'Yes, it is,' Merton replied. 'He has changed his robe for a pair of trousers. The white robe would be too noticeable.'

The three conspirators—the vicar, Miss Monteith, and Old Ned—first looked all about, then began advancing toward the graveyard. It was noticed then that the two men were carrying shovels. Merton had expected Miss Monteith would be carrying a bag holding the bones of some long-dead animal wrapped in a perishing blanket, the whole to be placed in Meg's arms. He could not see any such bag, however.

How did they hope to get away with such a foolish scheme? It would be obvious to the fellows who dug Meg up that the grave had been recently disturbed. Of course they could claim they were innocent. Someone else had done it. To remove the remains of the child? Was that it? Yes, that was actually more clever than to plant animal bones, which would be easily recognized as such. By beating the official exhumers to the disinterment, they would cloud the issue so that the truth could never be discovered.

Merton lit a twist of paper with the tinderbox, shielding it with his back, and then set the fire to the wax butts of candles in the damp wood. E're long a small blaze caught and smoke began to rise from the fire.

The three figures continued advancing, taking a straight course to Meg's grave by the edge of the graveyard. It was Miss Monteith who first noticed the smoke. She stopped and pointed. 'What is that?' she demanded.

A figure with long blond hair, wearing a woman's nightdress that was just a little too small and carrying a doll swaddled in a serviette, rose eerily from behind the cloud of smoke and uttered a low moan that lifted the hair on Charity's arms even though she knew it was only Lewis.

The ghostly apparition pointed a finger at the vicar and said in a warbling falsetto voice, 'My son, do not do this wicked thing, or you will suffer for all eternity, as I, your poor mother, suffer.' The vicar dropped the shovel and stared, his mouth hanging open.

The apparition continued. It pointed at Ned next. 'Ned, if you love me and our son, stop him from this dastardly deed.'

It was Ned who caved in first. 'Meggie! Is it really you?' he asked in a hollow voice.

'Silence, you fool!' Miss Monteith ordered. 'It is a trick. That demmed ghost hunter is behind this. They cannot possibly know the truth.'

'She's right,' the vicar said in a quavering voice.

Ned began blubbering. 'I'm scared, son. It ain't worth the risk. We have done well enough off the Mertons all these years. It is wrong, what you made me do. I must see dear Meg one last time.' He began advancing toward Lewis, who disappeared behind the smoke cloud, coughing into his fist, and thence through the yews out of sight entirely.

Merton said in a low voice to Wainwright, 'Take Charity home now. I shall meet you there shortly.' Then he stepped forth to speak to the conspirators. 'I have three witnesses to your confession, folks. Shall we go into the vicarage and discuss your limited options?'

Lewis soon joined the Wainwrights. He was carrying the nightdress and the bonnet to which yellow wool had been attached. His eyes were watering from the smoke and he was still coughing. 'By Jove! It worked like a charm. I was afraid I could not speak for the smoke in my throat, but it added a nice otherworldly edge to my voice. You are a genius, Wainwright. Let us go on into the vicar's place to watch them grovel and apologize.'

'Merton will handle it,' Wainwright said. 'He will meet us back at the Hall.'

'Just like him to keep the best part to himself I'd best put out that fire first,' Lewis said. He stamped the smoldering faggots until they were extinguished.

Charity felt Merton's wish for privacy had a kinder motive. He did not want to put the miscreants on public display, subject to Lewis's outspoken gibes. She said, 'Did I hear Ned call St John "son"?'

'That you did,' Wainwright replied. 'I had a chinwag with Merton late last night when he came to my room. We sorted it all out. Lady Merton mentioned her surprise that Meg had delivered the baby so soon. She had thought she still had a few months to go, yet she mentioned that Meg was very large.'

'I see what you are getting at,' Lewis said. 'She was *enceinte* before she caught Papa's eye. Ned was the culprit. They let on it was Papa's

210

work, to weasel things out of him. Old Ned got his "perkizzits," and Meg hoped to get Papa to support herself and Ned's son in style.'

'Which he did,' Wainwright threw in. 'Or the son at least.'

'I shouldn't be surprised if the trollop planned to carry on with Ned at his hermitage. I mean to say, why else was he so anxious to camp on her doorstep? We are fortunate she did not lumber so with a dozen brats.'

'Be that as it may,' Wainwright said, 'their son is St John.'

'You mean Old Ned is St John's real papa?' Charity said, still trying to absorb this new twist in the story.

'Certainly he is,' Wainwright said. 'But old Lord Merton had no notion of it, which is why he got the St Johns to adopt him, to keep him nearby.'

'And this is how they repay Papa!' Lewis stormed. 'Upon my word, hanging is too good for them. They ought to be drawn and quartered.'

They continued discussing the affair over a glass of wine at the Hall until Merton returned nearly an hour later. He looked more disturbed than triumphant.

'That was a messy business,' he said, accepting a glass of claret. 'But at least it is done with. I have a letter written by St John and signed by them all, confessing to their crime. I shall give it to Mama tomorrow. She will not have to see any of them again.'

'I hope you ain't letting them off with a little scolding,' Lewis charged.

'Not quite that easily,' Merton said. 'They have lost their positions here. The St Alban's fund will be terminated. Of course it was St John's intention to get your whole ten thousand out of Mama, Lewis. That would have been enough for him to give up his calling and flit off to London. He never wanted to be a clergyman. That was Papa's idea. St John will be going to London to look about for a position. His aunt, Miss Monteith, will go to keep house for him.'

'And Old Ned?' Lewis asked.

'Old Ned remains, under less opulent circumstances than previously.'

'You ought to give him the boot as well,' Lewis said. 'We figured out he planned to go on seeing Meg. That is why he wanted that house in the woods.'

'That may have been his original intention, but as he has been there some three decades, I believe he does have a taste for solitude. And Papa promised him, you know...'

'Yes, but Papa did not know all the circumstances!'

Merton looked almost embarrassed at his generosity. 'He is an old man, Lewis. Where would he go? What would he do? He will be no trouble. He was more a pawn in the game than anything else.'

Wainwright sipped the claret and said, 'I wonder what it was that set them off. Why, after all these years, did they decide to cut themselves in on a larger share of your estate at this time? Something must have happened, eh?'

'I believe they had been hatching the scheme for some time,' Merton replied. 'St John set up that St Alban's fund half a year ago, with a view to trying to get Mama to leave her fortune to it, with himself in charge of disbursing the funds. I looked over the paper I had foolishly signed. He, as president, had total control of the money. My signature was not required to cash a check.'

'I thought it was fishy all along,' Lewis said.

Merton continued. 'It was Miss Sabourin's pending retirement that brought the matter to a head. Monteith knew Mama's conscience was bothering her. She, Monteith, used that as a lever to ingratiate herself and get that position as companion. She was constantly on hand to keep Mama's guilt at the boil. The Hall has a history of ghosts. Why not add Meg to the retinue? The ghost of Meg was more likely to heat up Mama's guilt than anything else. Monteith admitted to the stuffed dummy on a string and the steam that came from the clothespress.'

'And the white bird?' Charity asked.

'That, too. She slipped into Mama's room while she slept, opened her curtains, and set the dove loose. It was also Monteith who helped

213

herself to your shawl, Charity. She was unhappy with Mr Wainwright's failure to find a ghost in Mama's room. She wished to discredit him and you in the hope that I would send you both packing.'

Wainwright shook his head. 'A dreadful woman. I sensed it the moment I laid an eye on her.'

'That is true,' Merton said, a frown pleating his brow. 'I believe you do have some power to read a person's character. A living person's, I mean.'

'And a dead person's, too,' Wainwright added, unhappy with this faint praise.

'Papa has many talents,' Charity said, smiling at her father. 'He told me I would not need my riding habit and there has been no occasion to wear it.'

'He also suggested you would need a party frock, *nest-ce pas*?' Merton added. 'That, too, was correct. We have been very remiss in entertaining you. Tomorrow we shall plan our rout party.'

Wainwright had no interest in rout parties. 'Very kind of you, Merton, but not at all necessary. We shall be leaving very soon now. It remains only for you to decide what you wish done about Knagg and Walter. If you want the antics in the Armaments Room to cease, then you must remove the yellow jerkin and the round helmet. If, on the other hand, you feel their presence adds a certain air to the house—

214

all the best houses have ghosts—then I suggest you place a good thick carpet under the table holding them, to prevent further damage to the helmet.'

'Perhaps that would be best,' Merton said. 'We would miss Knagg and Walter if they left.'

'You would still have your singing nun,' Wainwright pointed out. 'She will be with you for a while yet. Perhaps I could have a word with her and discover whatever became of Brother Francis. But I see you are looking fagged, Merton. Tomorrow will be soon enough. We shall say good night now. Come along, Charity.'

Charity rose and made her parting curtsies.

Merton disliked to do his courting in public. He bowed and said, '*A demain.*' With luck he should have his reply from Lord Bath tomorrow.

CHAPTER EIGHTEEN

It was a much-rejuvenated Lady Merton who met her guests the next morning. Merton had been to her room to show her the letter and to explain the situation. She even came to the breakfast table, a thing she had not done for months. With her cheeks carefully rouged and wearing an elegant mauve lutestring gown, she looked a decade younger than the lady who had first welcomed the Wainwrights to Keefer Hall.

She turned a doting eye on Wainwright. 'John tells me it was you who figured it all out. I knew the moment you arrived you would be my salvation. Do you remember? You looked deeply into my eyes and said, "Fear not, Lady Merton, we shall clear up that past transgression that is troubling you. It was not entirely your fault." I was at fault, too, of course. I dealt harshly with Meg, but I do not feel I deserved the shabby treatment I received. How did you know?'

Wainwright assumed a wise expression and a pontificating tone. 'There was a certain aura about you, a sadness greater than should have been there. I cannot explain how I know these things. It is a gift. Merton will tell you I pegged Miss Monteith for the culprit the minute I laid eyes on her.' He was never slow to blow his own horn. They both ignored her ladyship's period of displeasure with him.

'That is true, Mama.' Merton smiled. He had been begging his mother for weeks to be rid of Monteith, but this was not the moment to mention it. 'Mr Wainwright also insisted there was no ghost in your chamber, if you recall.'

'The ghosts were in my head,' she said. 'But they are gone now. I feel like having a party to celebrate. You must not leave until we have had a celebration, Mr Wainwright. I insist.'

216

He was putty in the hands of an admiring lady. Until the post arrived and Bagot handed him a letter, he discussed their mutual ghostly experiences at Keefer Hall, using this audience to see how his monograph for the Society would go over. The letter was not franked. It appeared to have been delivered by hand. Knowing of no other haunted house in the neighborhood, he did not expect an invitation to practice his calling and was therefore not much interested in it.

'What can this be?' he asked, slitting open his letter. A look of dazzled bliss settled on his face. 'From the Marchioness of Bath,' he said, his chest expanding with pleasure. 'She has asked me to take a run over to Longleat next week. How could she have known I was here? Lady Montagu!' he exclaimed. 'I mentioned in a note to her that you had invited me, Lady Merton. She knew where to find me. Most kind.' He glanced quickly through the missive. 'Ah, not Lady Montagu. I have you to thank, Merton.'

'I dropped Bath a note,' he admitted. 'As you have been such an inestimable aid to us, I took the liberty. I hope you do not mind.' He hardly felt it a liberty after Wainwright's hints.

'I am pretty busy,' Wainwright said, 'but I cannot deny such a plea as this. The Green Lady is acting up. It would be the new moon.'

Merton figured the marchioness had done him proud in her request. He must remember to write and thank her.

'There you are then!' Lady Merton exclaimed. 'You are halfway there. There is no point returning to London. You shall remain here over the weekend and continue on to Longleat next week.'

'My daughter will not be happy with me, I fear.' He looked at his daughter but saw only joy. 'She is always anxious to get home to her friends. But perhaps she will bear with me just this one more time. Longleat! Well, well. I shall be happy to meet the Green Lady.'

He glanced out the window. 'Ah, there is one of the ravens flying about the windows.'

'They do fly about from time to time,' Lady Merton said. 'It is only when they all take to circling the house in a frenzy that we expect good news.'

'There is another!' Lewis exclaimed. 'And another! Good God! What can it mean? Mama, you ain't *enceinte*—No, of course not.'

'They are announcing my recovery,' Lady Merton said as another black bird swished past the window. 'It is a sort of rebirth for me really. They flew like that when you were born, Lewis. What a tizzy they were in that day.'

'I believe I shall just go out and have a look at this phenomenon, if you will excuse me, madam,' Wainwright said, and rose. Lewis went with him, to inquire how he might expedite admission to the Society and which tailor had made the cape.

'Let us all go,' Lady Merton suggested. Merton pulled the ladies' chairs and they went out to view the circling ravens.

Charity and Merton lagged behind, then took a detour toward the far side of the house, stopping under the boughs of an apple tree.

Charity said, 'It was kind of you to write to Lady Bath. Papa is very excited.'

'Radley Hall must look to its laurels. Keefer Hall is nothing to it, but Longleat! Actually I wrote to Lord Bath, but it is the ladies who succumb to this sort of non—Er, to ghosts.'

'You still think this is all nonsense, don't you, Merton?'

'Seeing is believing. I have not seen a ghost yet.'

'You have heard the commotion in the Armaments Room.'

'And I have seen the dairymaid Lewis sent into my room. I have seen Old Ned wrapped up in your shawl, and I know Monteith dangled a dummy on a string to frighten Mama. That tells me these phenomena can be managed.'

'The Armaments Room was locked the last time the helmet and the jerkin were sent flying.'

'Well, perhaps ... But Bagot has a key.' He ducked as a pair of raven swept past his head, barely missing him. 'What would really convince me of earthly powers would be an announcement of a birth—or betrothal—in the family. As Mama is a widow, the ravens' flight must herald a betrothal.'

'Or a hawk attacking them,' Charity added prosaically.

'No, no. We are in the realm of romance here. Common sense is not allowed.' He seized her hands and turned her to face him. 'If you want to convince me there is anything in these legends of ghosts and ravens there must be a betrothal in the immediate offing.'

She saw the laughter in his eyes. 'What a sneaky trick, Merton!'

A raven settled on a bough of the apple tree and uttered an encouraging croak.

'You have hardly had time to hang up your hat. Are you not tired of all this darting about the countryside? If we were engaged, it would be unexceptionable for you to remain at Keefer Hall while your papa goes haring off to Longleat,' he explained.

She cast a flirtatious glance from the corners of her eyes. 'But Lewis has not asked me to marry him.'

'Wretch!'

'And naturally I could not accept any offer without Papa's permission.'

'I spoke to him last night. That is why I went to his room. After he expressed his delight in getting you off his hands, we spoke of other matters.'

'Delight! I have been a slave to him! Did he really say that?'

'No, he said he doubted you would be willing to give up your exciting life as his

220

assistant ghost hunter and amanuensis, but he gave me permission to ask.'

'It is certainly a difficult choice,' she said, feigning indecision.

'Charity! You implied you were unhappy darting from pillar to post.'

'Yes, but then would it be worse, living with a tyrant?'

'You know the secret,' he said, drawing her into his arms. 'You have only to ask for more than you want.'

Without further words he lowered his lips for a heady kiss. The raven uttered one more croak, then took to the air to join the other ravens in a frenzied circling of the house.

Neither Charity nor Merton was aware of the birds. They were lost in the rapture of their love as his lips bruised hers. Her arms moved uncertainly around his waist. Encouraged by this modest response, Merton crushed her to him until her lungs felt ready to explode and her head was spinning. Deep waves of joy battered at her until she felt inundated. A happiness greater than any she had ever known before washed over her. It was the sense of finally belonging somewhere, with a life of her own to live, with this man she loved.

After a long embrace, he released her and gazed bemusedly into her eyes trying to assimilate that this enchanting creature could truly care for him. 'You have just convinced me there are some things in this world beyond our

221

comprehension. I heard heavenly bells ringing.'

'Not heavenly. The bells came from the church. There is no service today, is there?'

'No. The change-ringers must be practicing. But how very mundane of you to bring me crashing to earth in this manner, my sweet. It is my job to rob an occasion of its mystery and romance.'

'No, just its mystery. I am too much my father's daughter to be robbed of romance.' She looked about for the ravens. They had ceased their flight and settled in a row on the roof of the Hall.

'Look, Merton! They have gone to roost.'

'Their job is done—until we have a birth in the family to set them off again. I hope to see them flying every year.'

'Every year! I hope you are asking for more than you want.'

'I only want you.' He looked at the row of ravens, who seemed to be staring down at him. 'You would not want to break the legend, Charity.'

'You do have some belief in that legend, do you?'

'Certainly,' he said firmly. 'It has always been so at Keefer Hall.'